MASTER OF KUNG FU

Cruelly orphaned at the age of twelve, Yi Wan is taken into the household of Li Su, one of the greatest martial arts masters in western China. The year is 619 AD, when the great Tang dynasty is ushering in a period of stability after the Korean Wars. Yi Wan is encouraged to study to become a doctor of acupuncture, but his real interest is in the style of Kung Fu taught by Li Su. He is privileged to spend a year at the famous Shaolin Monastery, learning their style of boxing, but on his return he finds that he has lost the girl he loves. In despair, he sets out for the capital, Chang-an, where he encounters corruption and violence, but also finds true friends and love of a sort. His return to western China brings sorrow, but ultimately the highest joy.

MASTER OF KUNG FU

E.G. BARTLETT

ROBERT HALE · LONDON

ISBN 0 7090 4633 2

Robert Hale Limited
Clerkenwell House
Clerkenwell Green
London EC1R 0HT

Photoset in North Wales by
Derek Doyle & Associates, Mold, Clwyd.
Printed and bound by Interprint Ltd.,
Valletta, Malta.

Part 1
TUNHUANG

One

Yi Wan did not hear Master Su approach. When the tall man's shadow hid the sun, he scrambled to his feet, and would have fled, but Su stayed him with a gesture.

'You are hurt, boy,' he said. 'Why did you fight?'

'They were going to harm the kitten, master.'

Su nodded. He had watched child and kitten scrabbling for food in the garbage piled at the end of the lane.

'So you fought three of them?'

But it was not only courage that had impressed Master Su, but the compassion of one needy creature for another.

'Where do you live, boy?' he asked gently.

Yi Wan was silent, knowing he could be handed over to the authorities, without knowing exactly what this would mean.

'You do not need to be afraid,' Su told him. 'Have you no parents?'

Yi Wan shook his head

'They are dead, master.'

'Will you come with me? I am a doctor. I can dress your wounds.'

There was something so compelling in the tall man's invitation that Yi Wan suspected he would not have been allowed to refuse. There was also a dignity and a caring that inspired trust.

Yi Wan made an instant decision, and together they set off down the dusty street. He did not know at that moment that he was being invited into the house of Li Su, the greatest martial arts master in Western China.

7

Su's house was a substantial building in a pleasant garden, set back from the main road, and shaded by trees. Yi Wan did not know the name of the town he was in, but it was clearly an oasis, because of the water. From the garden, he looked up to high peaks in the south.

He did not have time to take note of his surroundings, however, as Su led him straight into the front room. It was a plain bare apartment, the floor covered by a woven carpet that provided the only colouring. The walls were covered with cabinets containing bottles. There was only a table, a chair, and an upholstered couch in the room, but by the standards of seventh century China, it was a luxurious apartment.

'Lie on the couch, boy,' Su told him, and when Yi Wan had climbed up and lay flat, Su took off his hat and outdoor coat and came forward to examine him. Soft fingers, gentle as a woman's but with an iron hardness behind them, probed his chest and abdomen, and moved down to his limbs.

'Nothing is broken,' Su said, 'though you are badly bruised. I will give you a salve.'

The ointment he applied came from one of the bottles, and as he massaged it gently into the black and blue areas, Yi Wan felt warmth take away the soreness. Not until the treatment was complete did Su question Yi Wan further.

'Now tell me your name?' he said.

'Yi Wan, master.'

'You do not live in this town. Your speech betrays you. What have you done? Run away from home?'

Although all his instincts were against trusting anyone, Yi Wan had the feeling that it would be impossible to deceive this man. His eye pierced appearance to the truth behind appearance. He had a mystical almost frightening presence, as if his knowledge and his powers were above human understanding. But he had been kind. If he had wanted, he could have called the civil guard and handed Yi Wan over for creating a disturbance or for simple vagrancy.

'I was being taken to Persia in the camel train. I had heard what that would mean. I crept out of camp in the night, and hid until my captors gave up searching and moved on.'

'How old are you?' Su asked.

'Twelve, master.'

Su nodded his head thoughtfully. He too knew what kind of life a good-looking boy of that age would have been taken into. At the other end of the Silk Road there were brothels that catered for all tastes and perversions.

'Sit on the chair, Yi Wan,' he said, and taking his own seat on the couch, he proceeded to bring out the boy's story.

'What part of China do you come from?'

Yi Wan did not appear to understand at first, and Su realized that he had no idea of geography.

'How long were you with the camel train?' he pursued, re-phrasing the question.

'Thirty-two days, master.'

'Did you come from the south? From the sea?'

Yi Wan shook his head, and Su knew it must have been from the north-east.

'What did your parents do?'

'They were farmers, master.'

'And when did they die?'

'This year, master. In the War. Our own soldiers killed them. The Koreans were driving our army back. The soldiers looted the village. All who resisted were flogged to death or died by the sword. My whole village was wiped out, but they kept me alive and took me south with them to a big city. Here they sold me to a trader who was setting out for the west. I would have been his slave.'

'The trader was not Chinese?'

'No master.'

Although, in his own village of Tunhuang, Su was far distant from the war with Korea, news of it had come to him via the merchants and priests who travelled the Silk Road. The Nung, the peasant farmers, had borne the main burden of that ill-fated war. Their young men had been conscripted; their granaries emptied to provide fodder for troops and their horses; their villages laid waste by ill-disciplined troops returning starving from the fighting lines. It was still only a few days since news had come that General Li Yuan had become Emperor of China, and taking the name of Tai-Zong had put an end to the Sui Dynasty and founded the Tang Dynasty. It was the year AD 619, and there was at last hope that the wars were over, and that the new Emperor would behave as a true ruler, bringing stability, plenty and a benevolent rule, which was his Heavenly duty according to the Confucian ethic.

Li Su's benevolence sprang not only from the Confucian idea of duty, however, but from the Tao-ist belief in the harmony of nature and the Buddhist teaching of peace and right living.

'Would you like to stay with me, Yi Wan?' he asked. 'You are a free man. You can say "yes" or "no," but do not answer at once. I will take you to my cook. She will give you a meal and a place to sleep this night, and in the morning you shall tell me your decision. I am not offering you charity. I am offering you work. My gardener, Tai Do, is growing old. You shall help him and learn his trade, in return for your keep. If you prove yourself worthy, I will see that you receive an education that will enable you to take your place in the world, when you reach the age of maturity.'

Yi Wan could scarcely believe what he was being offered. When he had fled from the caravan and the life of slavery which he knew lay ahead of him, he had been prepared to beg his living if necessary. Now, he was being offered a home, more comfortable than his own had been, since in the poor soil just south of the desert his parents had only just scraped a living. He began to stammer his thanks, but Li Su held up his hand for silence.

'Never be hasty, boy,' he admonished. 'Tomorrow is the time for giving me your answer. Now is the time to eat.'

Taking Yi Wan through a long passage, he led him to the back of the house, where pots boiled on a huge open fire in the kitchen. A short stout woman bent over them, but straightened up at once and bowed as Li Su entered.

'This is Yi Wan, Xi Hang,' the master said. 'He is to be given a good meal, and then to be taken to the room over the stables. He will sleep there tonight, and you are responsible for his comfort. I shall see him in the morning, and we will speak further of the matter.'

Bowing as low as her ample figure permitted, Xi Hang answered 'Yes, master,' and a moment later, Yi Wan was left alone with her.

'Are you very hungry, Yi Wan?'

The cook spoke in such a strange dialect that Yi Wan did not at first understand what she was saying, and she repeated her question more loudly, as if she thought he was deaf. It seemed a stupid question to Yi Wan, anyway, since he had not eaten more than the scraps he could salvage from garbage tips for two days. This afternoon was the first time he had ventured out in daylight since his escape from the caravan. He had hidden in a cave outside the town at first, knowing that if he remained concealed for long enough the hunt for him would be called off. Traders on the Silk Road had to press on before their provisions ran out or Winter overtook them, and his captor would have assumed he had died in the desert. They would not come back after two days.

When Yi Wan had understood and answered the cook, she suddenly screeched 'Poppy!' in a voice so unlike her low guttural tone that it startled Yi Wan. To his amazement, a young girl answered the call, poking her head around the door of the kitchen. Yi Wan did not think she was any older than himself. Her small round face and black almond-shaped eyes under her fringe of black hair were all that he saw of her, but her beauty struck at his heart.

'Poppy,' the cook said. 'Get two blankets from the store room and a pillow. Take them and Yi Wan to the loft over the stable. He is to sleep there. Show him the couch and make up a bed.'

The girl disappeared.

'Your supper will be ready when Poppy has shown you where to sleep,' Xi Hang told Yi Wan.

He bowed, since this seemed to be the polite way of acknowledging any instruction in this household.

Poppy came back almost at once with the articles the cook had ordered clutched to her breast. She seemed so diminutive for such a burden that Yi Wan immediately took them from her, ignoring her protests.

'He will need a candle and a water jug,' Xi Hang said. 'Take these.'

Filling the jug and taking a candle lantern from a shelf, she gave them to Poppy.

'Do you know how to use tinder and flint?' she asked Yi Wan.

'Yes, madam.'

'Ma'am,' Xi Hang corrected.

The girl led him out of the kitchen, and into the garden at the back of the house.

'There are lavatories next to the stable door,' Xi Hang called after them. 'We are civilised here.'

Already the sun, which had been high enough to cast shadow when Master Su had found him, was sinking, and the air was turning chill. The desert night would soon close in. The garden through which they passed was strange to Yi Wan. It was divided into terraces and plots, and full of unusual plants, each labelled with its name on a wooden plaque. Yi Wan had been taught to read at his village school. His parents wanted him to become a teacher and to escape the drudgery of farm life which had been their lot. He did not know these plants, however, even though he could read their names.

Poppy walked quickly, and Yi Wan had almost to run to keep up with her. She was slightly shorter than he was, and she had the graceful movements that belong to the young. He wanted to ask her who she was, and what was her position in the household, and whether she was happy, but shyness held him back. He did not want her to think him forward, and was surprised that it should concern him what a girl might think of him.

At the end of the garden, they passed through a door in the mud wall, and came into a courtyard, on the far side of which was the stable block. Poppy struggled with the heavy door, until Yi Wan laid down the blankets and helped her. There were four horses in the stable, munching hay in their stalls. In the dim light, Yi Wan saw the ladder at one end that led to the loft. Poppy preceded him up it, and they came out into a large area, with a low sloping roof which reached the floor at the sides of the building. A slatted door at one end admitted some light. Much of the floor space was taken up with hay and straw, and bags of what looked like beans, but at the end nearest the door, Yi Wan saw that there was a wooden shelf with a straw palliasse on top, and beside it an earthenware bowl for washing.

'Here you are,' Poppy said. 'I will leave the lantern downstairs just inside the door, for when you come to bed. Now if you will go back to the kitchen, I will make your bed.'

These were the first words she had spoken to him, and Yi Wan was transfixed with joy at the music in her voice. He could hardly find words to answer, beyond stammering 'Yes' and 'Thank you.'

Descending the ladder, he found the lavatory, and feeling more comfortable, he returned to the kitchen, just as Xi Hang was ladling a mound of rice and chicken stew onto a plate.

'Sit here,' she said, and placed the steaming dish and two chopsticks in front of him.

The savoury smell reminded Yi Wan of his hunger.

'Well, start,' Xi Hang told him. 'Don't let good food grow cold.'

When he had begun to eat, she brought him a mug of water.

'There is wine if you prefer,' she said.

Yi Wan shook his head. He knew that wine took away the senses, and he wanted to be in possession of them all tonight, to savour the good fortune that seemed to have come upon him. This was food such as they had seldom been able to afford at home on the farm. Remembrance of home and of his parents brought tears to the back of his eyes, but he fought them back, turning his mind to the present to block out his memories of horror.

Poppy came in as he was eating, and slipped noiselessly through the door to some inner chamber where she doubtless lived. Xi Hang continued her work at the stove and at a table under the window.

Suddenly a faint sound came through the open door that led into the garden, and Yi Wan looked up. The kitten he had fought to save stood on the step, sniffing the air tentatively, before mewing again. Yi Wan was sure it was the same one, because he recognized the white apron on its black front, and the way three of its paws were white and one black. It had followed him, recognizing with an animal's instinct the first human who had shown it kindness.

Yi Wan's first impulse was to take a piece of chicken from his plate and to share it with the kitten, but Xi Hang foresaw his intention.

'Not in my kitchen.'

The words came out so fiercely that even the kitten was frightened. It shrank back.

'Please,' Yi Wan wanted to ask, 'may I not give him a little?' but before he could speak, the cook had moved to the stove, and was noisily clattering her pots and dishes.

'If you want to feed your cat, do it in the barn,' she said, suddenly thrusting a dish of meat scraps before him. 'If you have finished, you can do it now, and be sure to give him fresh water to drink with it. Cats get thirsty as well as hungry. Here, you'll need this second dish.'

Yi Wan was overwhelmed with relief that Xi Hang had such kindness in her heart.

'Wait, Yi Wan,' she said. 'Do you know what the great Lord Buddha did, in one of his lives on earth?'

'No, ma'am.'

'It is said that he came across a tigress in the forest with cubs playing around her, and seeing that she was too weak to find food either for herself or them, he went up to the top of a cliff, and threw himself down at her feet, thus giving her his own body to feed upon. This was the act that earned him Enlightenment, and this is why we too must be compassionate, Yi Wan. Is this the same kitten that Master Su told me you rescued?'

'Yes, ma'am, I am certain. Will I be able to keep him? I promise he will stay in the stable with me and not enter the kitchen.'

'You are going to stay then?'

'Of course. And can I keep the kitten? Will he be mine?'

Xi Hang permitted herself one of her rare smiles.

'Don't be a fool boy,' she said. 'He will never be your's, but you are already his, and he's demanding that you feed him now.'

Two

When Yi Wan awoke in the morning, a small old man was standing by his bed, holding a towel, soap and a dish which had already attracted the kitten's attention.

'Cook sends breakfast for your cat and says you are to come to the house immediately you have washed and dressed.'

Yi Wan was alert at once, and the clamour set up by the kitten reminded him that he had taken on responsibilities.

'Are you the gardener?' he asked.

'Yes. My name is Tai Do. Feed the kitten now before he claws my legs to pieces trying to reach the dish.'

Yi Wan took the plate and set it before the hungry animal. It was so thin that its bones seemed to stick out, and with loud purring it set about the meat ravenously. Yi Wan did not know how cats seemed able to purr and eat at the same time, but they all did.

'There is water for washing in the jug,' Tai Do said. 'Do not be long. The Master wants to see you after breakfast and he has a busy morning ahead of him.'

With a litheness that Yi Wan would have thought beyond an old man, Tai Do climbed down the ladder and began cleaning out the stable. Eager not to give offence, he hurriedly washed and dressed.

There was no sign of Poppy at the house, but the cook was waiting for him, and after enquiring how he had slept, she put a dish of oats and a hunk of bread in front of him. Water was again his drink, but it was pure and fresh, unlike that which had come from his well at home.

'What is the name of this town?' he asked.

'Tunhuang.'

'When may I see Master Su?'

'When he sends for you. Now do not bother me, Yi Wan. I have dinner to prepare.'

Xi Hang seemed so flustered this morning that Yi Wan was afraid to ask any more questions. He was glad when Poppy appeared and said that Master Su was ready to see him. She led him to a large room opposite the one in which Master Su had treated him, and Yi Wan saw that Master Su was not alone. A tall lady dressed in a silk kimono was also seated at the table. Su beckoned Yi Wan forward.

'This is Yi Wan, of whom I spoke to you, Wu,' he said. 'Yi Wan, this is my wife, Wu Su.'

Yi Wan bowed and the lady inclined her head. Yi Wan saw that her hands were small and they were not roughened with work as his mother's had been. She wore several gold rings on her fingers, and her hair was piled high over her head, as Yi Wan had once seen in the streets of Changan.

Clearly Master Su and his wife had been breakfasting, and Su now turned from the table to face Yi Wan.

'Well,' he said, 'have you reached a decision?'

'Yes, master,' Yi Wan answered at once. 'I would like to stay and work for you.'

'You know exactly what this means? You will do as Tai Do instructs you. You will take your meals with him in the kitchen. You will sleep over the stable. You will learn to care for the horses, as well as to assist in the garden.'

'And may I keep the kitten?'

Both Master Su and Wu Su smiled.

'Yes,' Su answered. 'You may keep the kitten.'

Master Su clapped his hands once, and Poppy appeared as quickly as if she had been waiting behind the door.

'Take Yi Wan to Tai Do and tell him the boy is staying.'

To reach the garden they had to pass through the kitchen, and Xi Hang glared at them as if they had no right there.

'Is cook always cross like this in the mornings?' Yi Wan ventured to ask Poppy.

'No,' she answered. 'It is her time of month.'

Seeing Yi Wan's bewilderment, she laughed.

'Don't you understand?' she asked. 'About women and their monthly flow?'

Yi Wan was embarrassed that he had forgotten how his mother had suffered, and how sometimes she had been unable to work in the fields. Of course he knew about women. He had lived too close to nature to be unaware of the facts of life.

To cover his embarrassment, he asked Poppy what her position was in the household.

'I am a bond-servant,' she answered. 'My parents have sent me to work for Master Su, in payment of debts.'

'And will you ever be free again?'

'When I am twenty-one, or when I marry.'

'And will you marry?'

Poppy laughed merrily.

'What a foolish question! How should I know? My parents will make arrangements, perhaps.'

'Do you like it here?' Yi Wan asked.

'It is a good household in which to work, most of the time. Master Su is gentle and good, and Mistress is fair. Cook is grumpy, but she has a kind heart.'

'Why then is it only good sometimes?'

'When Pei comes home it is not so good.'

'Who is Pei?'

'Master Su's son.'

'Is he unkind to you?'

But at this point, Poppy clearly felt that she had said enough, and she answered 'There is Tai Do.'

The gardener was bent over a strip of earth sheltered by the wall of the stable yard. Poppy took Yi Wan to him, and relayed Master Su's message.

Tai Do straightened up.

'You are ready to begin now?' he queried.

'If you wish, Tai Do,' Yi Wan answered politely.

'Come into the stables,' Tai Do said, and Poppy ran back to the house.

'Do you know anything about horses?' the old man asked.

'No,' Yi Wan admitted.

'But your people were farmers, were they not?'

'We had a bullock to draw the plough. We kept chickens and goats, but we never owned a horse.'

'These are fine animals, thoroughbreds, but they are temperamental and nervous of anything unusual. You must be careful when cleaning out or watering them.'

As they were talking, Tai Do led Yi Wan down the line of stalls.

'I shall be with you the first few times when you attend to them,' he said, 'and you need not be afraid, as long as you don't make any sudden movement to alarm them. But watch this.'

He edged himself between a horse and the side of a stall, and immediately the animal moved over towards him, so that Yi Wan was afraid he would be pinned against the side and crushed, but with a smile, Tai Do reached under the horse's belly and touched the animal on the far side. At once the horse moved away towards the hand that had touched him.

'If you remember this, you can safely go into the manger. They do not mean to crush you. They simply move towards what they feel at their side.'

Tai Do was not much taller than Yi Wan and of slight frame, but he was muscular. His skin was hard like leather, but it was not wrinkled as Yi Wan would have expected an old man's to be.

'Now I will show you the well,' he said, taking Yi Wan into the courtyard again. 'We take water to the house in the morning, sufficient for the day. We use this shoulder yoke to take two buckets at a time. We also have to water all the plants daily, because although we live in an oasis, the air is always dry.'

'Do you live in the house?' Yi Wan asked.

'No, in the cottage behind the stables. Through that door and down the lane.'

'By yourself?'

'Yes, my wife has been dead these ten years.'

'I am sorry,' Yi Wan said.

'One accepts. Xi Hang is my daughter. She has a different name because she is widow. Her husband died too.'

They came to a door in the side wall.

'Where does that lead?' Yi Wan asked.

'Ah that is not for you,' Tai Do answered. 'It is a forbidden place. Come into the garden.'

Pointing to one of the labelled plants, Tai Do asked, 'Can you read?'

'A little. That is Thyme, and that Fennel.'

As they proceeded round the garden, climbing the terraces and descending to the floor of the garden, Yi Wan counted a hundred and three different plants. Many of them were strange to him.

'They come from all over the world,' Tai Do said. 'We have rich soil here and anything will grow. These are medicinal plants that Master Su uses. You know he is a doctor?'

'Yes, he treated my bruises.'

'And how are they this morning?'

Yi Wan was amazed to realize that he had forgotten them.

'Master Su practises herbal medicine, but he is also an acupuncturist. Do you know what that is?'

'Yes, treatment by needles.'

'He is very famous and very good,' Tai Do said, speaking with pride because he was in the service of such a good man.

'And is his son a doctor?'

'Who spoke of his son?'

'Poppy told me he has a son who is away.'

'Pei Su is in Changan. You know where that is? The capital of China. He is studying at the University to enter the civil service. You will rarely see him.'

'Is he older than Poppy?'

'Older than you or Poppy. He is twenty-two.'

Their tour of the garden completed, Tai Do set Yi Wan to work at weeding the beds where herbs were growing. It was back-breaking work, bending over the hoe, careful not to damage the plants, ruthlessly tearing out the tough choking weeds. When the sun reached its height, the heat was almost unbearable, and Tai Do brought Yi Wan a straw hat.

'Wear this,' he said, 'or you will not last the day. And do not kill yourself. There is plenty of time. Gardening is a work of patience and love.'

At midday, they had a meal in the kitchen and rested an hour before resuming work. At five in the afternoon, they were called for tea, and the working day was over.

Yi Wan noticed that Tai Do did not have much to say to Xi Hang, even though she was his daughter. They ate for the most part in silence. The cook remembered that Yi Wan had a kitten, however, and after the meal, she gave him a packet of scraps to take over to the stables.

'Do not give them to him all at once,' she advised. 'A little now, and a little in the morning. It does not hurt a cat to be hungry sometimes. Then he will learn to catch mice and rats. Even a kitten must earn his keep.'

When Yi Wan thanked her, she said, 'Wait here a moment. I have something else for you.'

Instead of shouting for Poppy, she went into an inner room and brought out a pile of garments.

'These belonged to Master Pei, when he was your age,' she told Yi Wan', and mistress says I am to see if any will fit you. You will need a change of clothes and it is a pity to discard good ones.'

As she held garments against him to try them for size, Yi Wan was grateful again for all that was being done for him. At home, he had never had a change of clothes. He went to bed when his mother needed to wash what he wore, and he did not have new garments until the others were beyond patching. In a few minutes he had been fitted out with two pairs of trousers and four shirts, and had tried on sandals until he had found a pair that were reasonably comfortable.

'Now change your clothes once a week,' Xi Hang told him. 'And bring me the dirty ones to be sent to the laundry. And if you are not a happy lad tonight, you ought to be.'

Lying on his bunk, later that evening, Yi Wan thought that of course he was happy. He wondered, however, what he would do when his working day was over. Would he be allowed to go into the town? Could he talk to Poppy? That would be best of all. She was such a lovely girl.

Gradually, he became aware of unusual sounds coming from behind the door that Tai Do had said was forbidden to him. They sounded like the clack of wood on wood, and were punctuated by piercing screams.

He went to the door of his loft, from where he could look over the wall. There was a large building the other side, and if he listened carefully, he could catch the swish of feet on a polished floor. It sounded as if some violent activity was going on, and if he had not known that this house was a place of peace and love, he would have thought someone was being beaten in there. It was a disturbing thought.

Three

Yi Wan had been working with Tai Do for three months when Master Su next sent for him. Autumn had given place to Winter, and there was snow permanently on the mountains behind the town. During that time, good food and hard physical toil had developed his body, and he was now fully an inch taller and firm-muscled. The nights had grown colder, and Xi Hang had sent him extra blankets for his bed, a jacket to wear by day, and a thick curtain to cover the slatted door at the end of his loft. His kitten had grown into a cat, and although playful and friendly in the loft, which it regarded as home, it had become a hunter as soon as it stepped outside, and now spent whole nights roaming the area.

During those months, Yi Wan had learnt more about the town which was now his home. It was not big enough to be the provincial capital – that honour belonged to Po-yang, a town some forty miles to the east – but it was home to thirty thousand people, and there were scattered farms to the south, going back into the foothills. Most of the people worked in the silk industry, though a few were weavers or potters. The town lay on the Great Silk Road just before the point where it divided to skirt the Taklamakan desert. From here, merchants had the choice of either taking the northern route or the southern. Either way they escaped the full rigours of the desert. Camel trains frequently passed through the town, and there was considerable trade, both in the goods the townspeople manufactured and in farm produce, which travellers bought to top up their supply for the next stage of their journey.

Yi Wan had been taken into the town by Poppy on shopping expeditions, and had carried the heavy baskets of produce from the open-stalled market back to Su's house, but this had always been done during the hours of daylight. Tai Do had warned him that it was not safe to venture into the town at night. There were thieves, and revellers from passing caravans who made the night rowdy; there was the danger of kidnap, and worse unspecified dangers.

He had solved the mystery of what went on in the room behind the forbidden door. It was the training hall of the martial arts students. Master Su had forty full-time students who practised there daily. They came from a wide area, and stayed in various hostelries in the town, during their course of study. They were the sons of wealthy men. Master Su also accepted the child of a poor man, occasionally, if the child was exceptional and if, in his opinion, both child and parents were worthy people.

'Can I learn Kung fu?' he once asked Tai Do.

' "Kung fu" means serious study,' was the answer. 'The art they study is properly called "Wu Shu". But not yet.'

From the time he had asked, however, Tai Do would sometimes take a playful swipe at Yi Wan, which the boy learnt to duck. If he succeeded in doing this, and in also avoiding the follow-up blow or kick, Tai Do would laugh. Tai Do never landed these blows or kicks; they were the play movements of childhood. But he was so adept at them that it was clear to Yi Wan that the gardener had received some training. He wondered if he had studied under Master Su.

During these months, there had been changes affecting all the people. The Emperor, Tai Zong, had consolidated his position, bringing the benefits of firm rule to all the regions. He had divided his kingdom into provinces, with regional governors chosen from the civilian population. Power had shifted away from the military. Peace was restored with neighbouring countries, and learned men were being recruited into the government. With the growth of the new civil service, Master Su hoped his son would have a better chance of securing a post.

News of these changes only reached Tunhuang by word of mouth from travellers on the Silk Road, and they were all purely academic as far as Yi Wan was concerned. He did not concern himself with politics. That was for his elders.

When Master Su next called him to the consulting room, he hoped that Tai Do had told the master of his desire to learn Wu Shu, the martial art, but it was something quite different that Su had in mind for him.

'Sit at the table under the window,' Su said. 'I have something to show you.'

When Yi Wan had taken his place, Su produced a rolled-up chart from a cupboard, and came to stand beside him.

'Tai Do tells me that you have learnt all the names of the plants,' he said. 'You have been diligent. It was never my intention that you should remain a gardener. Your parents made sacrifices to see that you learnt to read. It is my wish to further their ambition for you. Do you know what this is?'

Master Su unrolled the scroll, and Yi Wan saw that it was a chart of the human body, with various points marked on it, connected by lines in various colours.

'I have never seen such a picture before, Master,' he answered.

'It is an acupuncture chart,' Su told him. 'The lines are called meridians, along which flow the life force. The dots are points at which needles are inserted to balance those forces. Without this balance, a patient falls ill. By restoring the balance we can make him better. Now there is a great need for healers in our country. I am the only doctor in a town of thirty thousand inhabitants. And your diligence and sympathy for the weak suggests to me that you could make a healer. Would you like to become one?'

Before Yi Wan could answer, Master Su went on.

'Take your time to consider. It is not an easy road. There are two ways into the profession. One is through the University. I was trained in Changan. That way of entry would not be open to you, unfortunately, but a man can also become an acupuncturist by apprenticeship. The training lasts six years. Think what it means. You will qualify just as you are reaching maturity, and you will have a useful life ahead of you. I shall also expect you to study herbal medicine, because sometimes one treatment is best, and sometimes the other. But do not answer lightly. Many who enrol at the University do not stay the course, nor is the profession of a doctor easy.'

Yi Wan was deeply aware of the nature of the opportunity that Master Su was offering him. Even in their wildest dreams his mother and father would never have thought he might train as a doctor. The most they had envisaged for him was to become a teacher in a rural school, or a junior post in the service of the area commander.

'I will be your apprentice, if you will have me, Master,' he said.

'You have answered wisely' Su told him, and then, as if he had read Yi Wan's mind, he added, 'but there is something else you want to ask me?'

'Yes Master. Tai Do says you are the greatest martial arts master in Western China.'

'There are some who would dispute that,' Su answered with a smile. 'I know that you are interested in the art, Yi Wan, but tell me: which is the better thing – to heal or to harm?'

'To heal, Master.'

'Then study that first.'

The next day, Yi Wan was taken off his work in the garden, and began work with Master Su. His first task was to prepare herbal medicines. The plants that he had previously known only as growing things now had to be treated in various ways. Some were dried and pounded with pestle and mortar to make a powder; some were soaked in alcohol to make a tincture; some had boiling water poured over them to make an infusion like tea; and others were actually boiled in water to make a decoction.

When Yi Wan had prepared and labelled a bottle, Master Su would tell him the purpose for which it was used. The bottles in Su's cabinet constantly needed replenishing, and sometimes Yi Wan made up a dozen different mixtures in a day. He would then try in the evenings to remember what each one was for, so that when Master Su tested him the next morning, he could give the right answers. During those early days, he did not see patients, but worked in a small cabinet just behind the room where Su received patients. Between consultations, Master Su would come and tell Yi Wan one or two basic facts about holistic medicine, and he learned how man fitted into the rhythms of nature.

This learning occupied him fully throughout the winter and early spring, and he had no time for anything else. When he met Tai Do, the old man would still playfully hit him, to test his reactions, but Yi Wan learnt to avoid these attacks instinctively, without even thinking about them.

He still saw Poppy occasionally, but she did not dine in the kitchen with them, taking her meals in her own room, which he learnt was on the ground floor behind the store room. He wondered if she was lonely, or ever regretted the fact that her childhood had slipped away in service, but she always seemed happy, and sometimes he would hear her singing to herself as she cleaned the house.

As well as absorbing the basic ideas behind acupuncture and studying the uses of herbal medicine, Yi Wan had to study the acupuncture chart Master Su had given him, and not until he had memorised all the three hundred and sixty five points did Su let him sit in on the treatment of a patient. It was an old man from the town.

To Yi Wan's surprise, Master Su did not immediately ask the patient what he was complaining of, but began to ask about his life history, and any worries or problems he encountered in daily living. They talked about the season of the year and the time of day, as if all this had some bearing on the patient's condition. Finally, Master Su made the man lie on the couch and relax for ten minutes, while he was taking his own pulse.

'All this is relevant,' he told Yi Wan, quietly, 'and the taking of our own pulse. We must do this before we take the patient's.'

Taking the patient's pulse occupied ten minutes. Su felt both wrists in turn, and was a long time making his diagnosis.

'Now before I treat you, may I ask a favour of you?' he said to the patient. 'Yi Wan is an apprentice of mine. I should like him to feel your pulses as well, so that he may learn. Have you any objection?'

'No doctor,' the patient responded, and Yi Wan saw that his master must be very highly regarded for permission to be given so readily.

Su turned to Yi Wan.

'Your own pulse, first.'

Yi Wan had a job to find that.

'Place your fingers thus and relax. Try to feel the beat. Can you? Now try with the patient. As he is a man, you take the left pulse first. With a woman it is the right one first.'

When Yi Wan had found the place, Master Su told him, 'Now press a little harder, and you will feel a deeper pulsation. Can you feel that?'

Again it needed several attempts, and Yi Wan could scarce distinguish the difference.

'It is something that only comes with long practice,' Master Su told him. 'There are three pulses that can be felt superficially, when your touch is light, and three more at a deeper level, when you hold more firmly. It is from these pulses and the qualities in them that we learn the nature of the patient's illness.'

Yi Wan was conscious that it would need a lot more practice and a greater sensitivity to touch than he had at the moment.

'Do not be impatient,' Su said, when he saw the boy's dismay. 'It comes with practice, like everything else.'

Yi Wan shrank from the insertion of the long needles into the man's body, imagining that he would feel pain, but Master Su assured him that there was no pain, and the patient showed no sign of discomfort. When he had gone, Su showed Yi Wan the various types of needle used, and explained their purpose.

The time he had spent on just one consultation told Yi Wan

more clearly than anything else the need for trained practitioners. With all the will in the world, Su could not treat more than eight or ten patients in a day. This forced Yi Wan to go on, even when he despaired of ever remembering all the things he was being taught.

In the Spring, when he felt especially despondent, Su told him to take a rest.

'Go shopping with Poppy again. Get her to show you the town. You will come back refreshed, and when you do. I will give you a book that you will need, the Nei Ching. It tells you all there is to know about acupuncture.'

Going out with Poppy again seemed a wonderful idea to Yi Wan. He had always wanted to know her better.

Four

Yi Wan knew that Master Su must have given instructions to the cook, because she readily released Poppy the next morning.

'I am to show you the interesting sights,' Poppy told Yi Wan. 'Which would you like to see first? The school? The market? Or the rock caves of the Buddhists?'

Yi Wan had already visited the market with Poppy many times, when he had carried back the heavy baskets.

'The caves,' he answered.

'They are a mile out of town.'

The roads on which they walked were all made of dirt, pressed hard by feet and the passage of camel trains. The town houses were all made of clay blocks and wooden frames, thatched with straw. All except Master Su's were single-storey. The shops were open-fronted like the market stalls, and at most of them traders sat outside and waited for custom.

They passed the square, leading off which was the lane where Yi Wan had first encountered the kitten. He had never since seen the boys who were going to harm it, nor did he think he would recognize them now. Both he and they were older. A little further on, Poppy pointed out the school.

'Did you go there?' Yi Wan asked.

'No. My parents did not have the money. I am not clever like you, Yi Wan. I cannot read.'

'Then I will teach you.'

'How can you? You will not have the time, and for what purpose? I will always be a servant girl until I marry.'

Yi Wan could not think of Poppy as a married woman. She was still a girl to him, though he had learnt that she was fully a year older. He made up his mind however that he would ask Master Su if Poppy might have lessons. He wanted her to have the advantage of education, and if he could teach her himself, it would bring them together.

'Where do your parents live?' he asked. 'In this direction.'

'No, to the east. Our farm is eighteen miles distant.'

'Do you never go home?'

'No. Who would take me? There are dangers outside the town limits. Wild beasts and sometimes bandits.'

'But we are going outside the town now.'

'Only a very short way.'

The road climbed a hill as soon as they passed the last house, and they walked over sand-dunes covered with a coarse grass. Ahead they could see a deep ravine, which led away into the distance. Poppy stopped to point out the road.

'That leads to the desert,' she said. 'The monks' caves are over there.'

Yi Wan had to follow her pointing finger very closely and to strain his eyes to see the openings in the face of what appeared to be a sheer cliff, and all the time, he was conscious of Poppy's nearness. Wooden platforms had been constructed outside the mouths of the caves to form a kind of balcony, and above them Yi Wan saw carvings in the sandstone of the cliff face.

'How do the monks get up there?' he asked.

'There are paths. See, one starts there. You can just follow it up the cliff.'

'And why do they live there?'

'They are holy men. Pilgrims and travellers climb up to them to ask a blessing or advice on their journey. All the trading caravans pass through this valley. Sometimes the monks come down with their begging bowls, and people give them food.'

Yi Wan was more interested at that moment in Poppy herself.

'How did your father become indebted, so that you have to work as a bond-servant?' he asked.

'Sometimes the summers are very dry. Then the crops fail. When this happens we cannot pay our taxes to the local lord. If I had brothers they would have been taken into the Army and would serve in place of taxes. As I have only sisters one of us must go into the service of someone who will be responsible for the debt. I was the oldest.'

'It is a harsh system.'

'It is just. The state must survive.'

'But don't you want to be free, Poppy?'

'Freedom is inside you.'

Yi Wan felt that this was something he had always known, even when he had been a captive.

'They are going to take you into the martial arts school,' Poppy told him later.

'How do you know this?'

'I hear many things, but do not say that I told you.'

'Does Master Su teach, himself?'

'Only the senior pupils. Tai Do teaches the beginners.'

'Tai Do?'

Yi Wan repeated the gardener's name incredulously. Tai Do was an old man to him. Then Yi Wan remembered how lithe and unwrinkled the gardener's body was, and how Tai Do had always been able to hit him if he wanted, even in play.

'Tai Do was one of Master Su's pupils himself,' Poppy explained.

'Why would they not let me join before?' Yi Wan asked.

'Many ask to join but few are accepted. Master Su and Tai Do have been assessing your worthiness. If your attitude had been wrong, you would have been rejected. But they are pleased with you.'

Whilst they had been talking, they had wandered along the top of the hill that looked down into the ravine on one side and back to the town and the flat plain beyond on the other. Yi Wan saw that the mountains to the south were nearer than he had thought and that the vegetation and trees extended half way up them. Above the tree-line, however, the mountains were bare rock, and they formed an unscalable barrier that cut off the country that lay beyond them.

All the time, Yi Wan was conscious of Poppy's fragile beauty. Her hands were so tiny that it was difficult to think of them doing hard work, either in the house or on the farm. Her head reached his shoulder, and she was so light he felt he could have picked her up with one hand. He longed to touch her, to take her hand in his, but she kept her distance from him, as if she knew his feeling. If he had dared, he would have taken her in his arms and kissed her, but he was afraid of destroying their friendship before it had begun to ripen. He felt that she must like him, however, because laughter was never far from her eyes, and she seemed happy to be walking with him.

Before he could say any more, Poppy said it was time to go back, and even though Yi Wan knew she would still be near him in the house, it was not the same as this nearness.

They did not go out together again, and on the morning when he renewed his studies, Su told him that they had decided to let him study the martial arts as well.

'It will be a good way of keeping fit,' Master Su told him. 'Working in the dispensary all day and then reading your charts and book all evening does not give a balance to your life. You need physical exercise to develop your body and to keep your mind fresh, and Wu Shu will lead to spiritual development as well.'

Yi Wan used the opportunity to ask if he could teach Poppy to read.

Su was surprised at the request.

'Does she want to learn?'

'I don't think so, but education opens doors, and is of value in itself. It enriches life.'

'Wisely spoken,' Su agreed, 'and of course in teaching you will improve your own ability. I will speak to my wife this evening.'

After the evening meal, Tai Do changed into his Wu Shu practice suit and took Yi Wan through the door to the dojo.

He had provided Yi Wan with similar clothes, loose jacket and trousers tied with a sash, and when they stepped into the hall, Yi Wan was surprised at how big it was. The room was at least a hundred feet long, and half as wide, and the floor was of polished wood. The walls were bare, and windows high up along the side let in light and air. There were no decorations apart from a slogan at one end that read 'Martial Art – Martial Virtue', and a picture of the Master at the other.

As soon as they stepped through the door, Tai Do stopped and bowed gravely and deeply, though it seemed to be to no-one in particular.

'We bow to the place,' he explained, 'because the hall where we practice is sacred to the study of the way. You must always bow, therefore, when entering or leaving the room.'

A group of boys who had been awaiting their coming now formed a straight line at one side of the hall.

'Go and join the right hand end,' Tai Do said. 'They are in order of seniority, and you must take your place at the end as a beginner.'

When Yi Wan had done this, Tai Do stood facing them. Without any instruction being given, they all stood for a moment, perfectly still and in silence, and then bowed to their instructor and he to them. The discipline impressed Yi Wan. He had only met boys in his home village before, and they were anything but still and quiet. The teacher often had a job to call them to attention. Yet here, discipline seemed to come from within each individual.

Their salutations over, Tai Do made them line up in rows.

'Spread out, so that you all have room,' he said. 'We are going to practice movements.'

He demonstrated what to Yi Wan seemed simply walking down the hall, but when he explained how it was to be done, with the knees slightly bent, without raising the hips, and with none of the up-and-down movement to a normal walk, and also without losing balance, Yi Wan found that it was harder than it looked.

'Keep your eyes to the front,' Tai Do ordered. 'Fix them on

an imaginary opponent. Remember he will attack you if you take your eyes off him, or if you are off balance. Keep your fists close to your hips, ready to parry or counter. Turn smoothly at the end of the hall. Come back down.'

They did each step to numbers which Tai Do called out, and as they practised, Tai Do would rush amongst them to point out faults and to show them they were off balance.

From walking, they proceeded to blocking imaginary attacks, and the whole evening's practice was taken up in this way. Yi Wan was disappointed. He had imagined the study would have consisted of fighting with other boys, even if blows were not landed.

'Is all practice like this?' he asked Tai Do, when they had left the hall.

'In the beginning.'

'But do we never fight?'

'You have not yet learnt to stand correctly. How can you fight, when you are off balance? Don't be impatient, Yi Wan. Everything will become clear in time.'

'Haven't I sometimes heard the clack of wood on wood?'

'Yes, that is the seniors practising with wooden staves, but you cannot go on to weapon training until you have mastered empty handed fighting.'

Yi Wan had thought the training easy, but when he awoke the next morning, he could hardly turn over in bed. All his muscles were aching, and he massaged them in disbelief, before he was able to get up and wash.

Su smiled when he presented himself at the treatment room.

'Feeling stiff?' he asked.

'Yes Master.'

'Now you know why you must begin with simple movements.'

Yi Wan's day now consisted of work in the dispensary or the treatment room, followed by an hour in the Wu Shu training hall, followed by acupuncture study in his loft, and at the end of a week, Su told him it had also been arranged that he should give Poppy reading lessons.

'You can spend half an hour with her, immediately after breakfast, before you come here and before she sets out for market. I will give you paper and brushes and ink. Teach her the simplest characters first, and do not be impatient with her. She will not learn as quickly as you do.'

Five

Later in life, Yi Wan looked back on his teenage years as a golden period, when it seemed that the sun always shone and a quiet happiness pervaded every aspect of his life. He forgot the difficulties and the times he almost gave up his studies in despair, but he never forgot how just being with Poppy enriched his days.

Master Su's house was not a big one, and Poppy had never been over-worked there. She rightly appreciated that she would have been worse off at home, where she would have been expected to help on the land as well as taking responsibility for her younger sisters and helping her mother through future pregnancies.

She made light of Yi Wan's wish that she should learn to read, at first, but seeing how earnest he was and that it seemed to be her mistress's wish as well, she accepted his tuition. They met in her room, which was a small apartment behind the store room.

Yi Wan had never been trained to teach, but he remembered the way the village schoolmaster had taught him, and he patiently explained to Poppy what each picture character meant, and encouraged her to reproduce the characters as she learnt them, with brush and ink. He was himself learning new characters from Master Su, as new and unfamiliar ideas had to be expressed in his medical studies, so that, to the four hundred or so characters he already knew, he was adding several more each week. He had been told that there were over two thousand characters to learn.

'But if she manages seven a week, that is good,' Master Su told him. 'How many years did you spend in school yourself?'

'Two, but not continuously. I could only attend in the winter months. In summer I was needed on the farm.'

The half hour lessons with Poppy passed all too quickly, and they were the highlight of Yi Wan's day. He had been an only child, and she filled the place in his life of the sisters he had never had. He loved her as he would have loved a sister, without any strong sexual element in his feelings. Indeed he was too absorbed in his studies and his teaching to respond to his developing sexuality. Wu Shu training and his medical studies absorbed all his energies. Sometimes he wondered if he would ever remember all there was to learn in both these fields.

Su was never impatient with him, and this helped Yi Wan never to be impatient with Poppy, whose dedication to study was very much less than his.

The martial art study became more interesting as he progressed. In his second year, he was familiar with all the blocks and kicks and blows, and at this stage he was allowed to spar with a partner. Tai Do impressed upon them that they must not land blows, however.

'We are not learning to hurt each other,' he said, 'but so that we may be prepared to face an outside aggressor.'

Just after Yi Wan's sixteenth birthday, Pei Su came home. Poppy's class was cancelled, and Yi Wan was disappointed, but he was interested in meeting the young man of whom he had heard. Pei Su did not put in an appearance until the afternoon after his arrival, however. Then he came into the treatment room.

He was as tall as his father, but rather more fleshy in his build, as though he were out of condition. Although according to what Yi Wan had heard, he would be about twenty-five or six, he looked more like thirty, and had the beginning of a paunch. His hair was beginning to recede, and Yi Wan could see that he would follow his father and become bald before he was much older.

From the few things that he had heard about Pei Su, Yi Wan had expected a loud-mouthed bullying type of fellow, but the young man knocked politely at his father's door and waited permission before entering the room.

'I have brought the model you required father,' he said. 'Shall I put it here?'

Master Su took the bundle from his son, and unwrapping it displayed a life-sized wooden figure of a man.

'Very good, Pei,' he said. 'Did you have difficulty in obtaining it?'

'I searched in several shops,' Pei answered. 'They said that I must have one made especially, but I was unwilling to go to that expense. At last I tried the University stores, and they were able to help out. When I said it was for you, they did not charge me.'

'Then I must write a note of thanks for you to take when you return.'

Although Yi Wan was present at this meeting, Pei Su took no notice of him. It was as if he did not exist, and Yi Wan saw that Pei considered him no more than a servant in his father's household. When Pei left the room, Master Su called Yi Wan to look more closely at the model Pei had brought, and Yi Wan saw that it was hollow and full of small holes.

'Each hole is one of the acupuncture points you have learnt,' Master Su told him. 'In the examination for your diploma, you will find a figure like this coated with wax and filled with water. The wax will hide the holes and prevent the water escaping. You will be asked to identify various diseases and to insert the needles at the correct points. If you find the hole immediately, the needle will slip in easily and water will flow, showing that you have found the right spot. If you fail to find the exact place, the needle will not go in. I asked Pei to obtain this model so that you might practise. When I am sure you are inserting the needles at the correct places. I shall ask you to do so with a patient.'

Yi Wan had a feeling that even if his parents were glad to see Pei Su, his presence in the house cast a shadow over the

others. Not only were Poppy's lessons suspended, but Xi
Hang grumbled because he did not eat at the same time as the
rest of the family, and once, after Yi Wan had seen Pei with a
woman of the town, he heard Tai Do say to the cook, 'That
boy will break his father's heart.'

A few days later, Poppy dared to interrupt the Wu Shu
class.

'Master Su says you are to come with Yi Wan, Tai Do.
Master Pei is hurt. He has crawled to the door, but Master Su
needs help to bring him inside.'

'Fetch a plank as a stretcher,' Master Su told Tai Do.

'What is it?' Yi Wan asked.

'He has dislocated his ankle,' Su answered.

When Tai Do returned, they rolled Pei onto the plank, and
with one at the head and one at the foot, they carried him to
the treatment couch. Madame Su appeared in the hall,
looking anxiously at them.

'Get Poppy to prepare his bed, if it is not already done,' Su
told her, 'and put in some hot water jars. He is in shock.'

'Now this is going to hurt,' Su said, 'and I want you both to
hold him down firmly.'

Stationing themselves on either side of the couch, Tai Do
and Yi Wan placed restraining hands on the patient. Master
Su caught hold of his right foot, and with a mighty twist and
thrust put the bone back in place. The pain was such that Pei
Su leapt up convulsively, despite their hold, then sank
immediately into unconsciousness. Whilst he was in that
condition, Su applied a bandage to hold the limb so that the
bone would not come out of joint again.

'Carry him to his bed,' he said.

It was a day later that Yi Wan heard what had happened.
Pei had got into a fight in the town. He was too drunk to know
what he was doing, and the other man had dislocated his
ankle with a side kick.

'It is a movement I have shown you in class,' Tai Do told Yi
Wan, 'so you can see why I caution you never to land blows or
kicks in practice. This is the effect they are intended to have.

But Pei's opponent was lucky. If Pei had been sober, he would have killed him.'

'Is he good then?' Yi Wan asked.

'He was one of his father's better pupils,' Tai Do answered.

The fact that there were no repercussions to the fight probably depended on Master Su's standing in the town. Brawls were not uncommon, but disturbance of the peace usually brought action from the civil guard. Nothing happened in this case, however, except that for weeks, the Su household seemed to revolve around Pei and his demands. Yi Wan thought that even his parents looked forward to the time when he would be well enough to go back to Changan.

Master Su began to contact the leaders of passing caravans, asking their destination, and as soon as Pei could walk again, he made arrangements for him to travel with a caravan going to the capital.

Pei showed no objection to leaving.

'I'm sick of this place anyway,' Yi Wan heard him say, and Yi Wan was sorry, realizing how Pei's attitude would hurt his father and mother.

On the day after Pei had left, Yi Wan went to Poppy's room to give her a reading lesson, and it was while she was writing with the brush that he noticed the bruises on her arm.

'How did you get these?' he demanded.

'I bumped my arm against a door.'

'And made four marks on one side and one on the other.'

Yi Wan's work in the treatment room had made him observant of any injury.

Poppy looked down at her work, ashamed that she had lied to him.

'Who did this to you?' he asked. 'Tell me.'

'Pei Su,' she said in a whisper.

'Why?'

'I used to take him his breakfast in bed every morning. You know that even before he was an invalid he did not get up till midday. He caught my arm and tried to pull me close. I resisted and he squeezed my arm, until I cried out. He let me go then, because he did not want his father to hear.'

'Why didn't you tell them?'

'And add to their sorrow. They are disappointed enough in Pei already.'

'Why didn't you tell me?'

'And have you fight him? He would have killed you, Yi Wan. Oh yes, I know you are improving in your studies, and Tai Do thinks well of you, but you are still a novice and Pei is a graduate. Before he first left home, Master Su thought Pei had the makings of a champion. You have yet to be promoted to the senior class. Don't think I am belittling you, Yi Wan. You just need more time.'

If nothing else would have made Yi Wan train hard, this incident would have determined him. Before he was twenty, he would be as good as Pei, or better.

Six

On Yi Wan's nineteenth birthday, he sat the test to become a teacher of Wu Shu. He had practised the martial arts daily for six years, and when he was promoted to the senior class at sixteen, he had doubled the hours he spent in training. During this time, he had grown to his full stature, and his muscles had become hard as iron.

This practice, with his medical studies, left him no free time at all, but he did not mind. Work protected him against memories of the terrible thing that had happened to his parents. Only two incidents stood out in all those six years, as far as Wu Shu was concerned. One was the day Master Su himself gave a demonstration with two of his senior pupils.

It was done in honour of a visiting celebrity, but although Yi Wan forgot who the celebrity was, he never forgot Master Su's incomparable skill. Until that moment, Yi Wan had thought Tai Do was good, but seeing a top master in action, even at the age of seventy or so, opened Yi Wan's eyes, and at the same time humbled him. Master Su's movements were like lightning. He defeated multiple assailants at once; he disarmed attackers who were using real weapons. He fought younger men with no sign of breathlessness, and for the first time, Yi Wan realized how far he had to go.

The second incident occurred two years later, when a big thickset Turk who announced himself to be a wrestler who was passing through with a caravan, asked if he might watch practice in the hall, together with his two sons.

Permission was given, and the three men sat quietly until the lesson was over.

'I see that you do not perform feats of strength,' the Turk said, at the end. 'Bring me an iron bar.'

When one was brought, he twisted it into a corkscrew around his forearm.

'Can anyone do that?' he enquired.

'It is purely a demonstration of strength, not part of martial art teaching,' Master Su told him.

'Then let one of your pupils attack me with a Club.'

The force with which he blocked the downward blow split the heavy Club in two. His strength was truly amazing.

'Now will anyone fight with my sons or with me?' he challenged.

Although Master Su's methods were gentle and did not encourage contests, it was traditional that if a challenge was issued, the Master had to put forward students to respond. Yi Wan was glad that he was a comparative junior and unlikely to be selected. He knew that he could not match the feats of the Turk, and his sons seemed just as powerful. He would have an opportunity now of seeing Master Su's best men in action.

Master Su asked for volunteers, and of the dozen who stepped forward, he chose three. Two of his best undergraduates were matched against the sons; a graduate was chosen to oppose the Turk.

The first two matches went evenly. The Turkish boys evidently depended chiefly on grappling techniques, which Master Su's boys easily evaded. Whenever the Turks took them to the floor, they broke free, using locks on the wrist or elbow to do so. After fifteen minute contests, their respective masters agreed to call it a draw.

Now it was the turn of the Turkish master himself and the young graduate. Yi Wan was anxious, because although he knew Master Su's pupil was good, he was only half the size of the Turk. To everyone's astonishment, not least the Turk's, he won the match in ten seconds, avoiding the Turk's rush and snapping his arm with a swiftly applied armlock.

'You must allow me to treat you,' Su said, at once. 'I am a doctor as well as a teacher.'

Humbled, the Turk agreed, and Master Su took him to the treatment room.

'I will arrange for your accommodation in the town if you wish,' he said, but the Turk was gracious, and said that he had his tents and that he must press on in the morning. 'Keep your arm in a sling,' Master Su told him. 'Do not take off the splints for three weeks. It will have set by then.'

Yi Wan expected the graduate to be congratulated on the ease with which he had won, but instead Master Su told him, 'That was an over-reaction. You were afraid of losing. You need not have broken his arm. You must never allow fear to determine your actions.'

'No master,' was the answer.

By incidents like these, Yi Wan learnt what high standards were required of masters, and when he came to the day of his own examination, he knew exactly what was expected of him.

The test for a teacher's certificate was in seven parts: basic exercises, movement, evasions and blocks, empty handed attacks, the use of staff and stick, the use of sword and dagger, including disarming an armed opponent, and finally an oral examination on the philosophy of Wu Shu. Five other men hoped to graduate on the same day as Yi Wan.

Yi Wan rose early, and went through the routine of suppleness exercises before he washed and dressed. Then, after a light breakfast, he presented himself at the hall. Poppy had washed his practice suit especially, because a grubby suit or late arrival would have been a discourtesy that would have led to automatic failure. His fellow students were also early.

Precisely at the hour appointed for the examination, Master Su came into the training hall, with Tai Do and another graduate who were to help in the examination. After exchanging bows with the candidates, they seated themselves on the raised platform at the end of the room.

There was a moment's silence, in which they had the opportunity to calm their minds.

Then Master Su said, 'We will take the preliminary exercises together. Line up across the hall. Show me Exercise one.'

The candidates were so placed that they could not watch each other's movements and so copy someone else. They each had to rely on their own memory of the sequence, but since this was strictly adhered to in every training session, they had done the exercises thousands of times, and did not find them difficult. Yi Wan kept his eyes strictly to the front. He was conscious of the man on either side of him, but he deliberately avoided thought of what they were doing.

'Now, movement,' Su commanded. 'Walk to the end of the hall and back, three times. I want correct stance, balance, and correct turnings.'

These were the movements that Tai Do had taught Yi Wan on his first day of training, but now he had to perform them perfectly. He remembered that on that first day, the slightest touch of Tai Do's finger was enough to put him off balance. His performance now must be as firm as a rock, because it was from this solid base that all the power in a kick or a blow would come.

At the end of this section of the examination, there was a pause, during which Master Su conferred with the other examiners, and they recorded the marks awarded to each candidate.

Now came the more difficult section of the examination: eight techniques of blocking attack to various parts of the body. For this, they were paired up, and the attack had to be genuine. A faked performance would instantly have stood out and disqualified both candidates. The attacks were fast; the blocks hard. Against an untrained man, even the block would disable. Each student was required to demonstrate evasion of the attack and then the block and counter. In this way they showed knowledge of attack and defence. Finally, in this section, they were asked to demonstrate blows, strikes, and kicks to various targets, identifying the target and making the attack without actually landing the punch or kick. This called for precise judgement of distance and for perfect timing, and since only one pair could demonstrate at a time, this part of the test took up all the rest of the morning.

'How are you getting on?' Poppy whispered at lunch time.

Yi Wan did not know, but he reassured her. It pleased him that she cared, but he did not allow himself to speculate on how well he was doing or otherwise. It was essential for him to be relaxed, since in the afternoon, he had to deal with attacks using weapons, and the only way to do so was to allow his instinct and his reflexes to take over. One of the first lessons he had learnt was that tenseness prepared a man to meet only one situation, the one he expected; relaxation enabled the body to respond freely to whatever the opponent did. He lay on his bed therefore after his meal, and steadied his breathing. Oxygen calmed the nerves.

In the afternoon, they were again paired up, and first demonstrated attacks with the staff and the stick. The former was a heavy weapon six foot long and capable of smashing bone if the blow was landed. The stick was of hard wood and could knock a man unconscious. Precise and controlled movement was therefore essential if they were not to land a blow and so disable the partner. Trust in the partner was also essential so that they accepted the attack without flinching, knowing that the other's judgement could be trusted. Parries and counter attacks followed; then free sparring, which demonstrated their instinctive knowledge of what the other man would do next.

Finally, they had to demonstrate the various movements possible with each of the traditional weapons. These were the chien or straight sword, the Kwan Do or halberd, the Chi'ang – a nine-foot spear, the Yue – a multi edged weapon, the piao or short dagger, the san cha or trident, and the rope which was used with a sharp edged weapon like the yue attached to the end.

The last test of all was for an unarmed man to take one of these weapons away from an assailant. Yi Wan needed all his calm and all his courage to do this. One slip or misjudgement by either partner could mean a finger or a limb sliced off. The secret was to come inside the attack, to grasp the opponent's wrist after the blade had passed, and by a painful lock against the elbow to compel the opponent to drop the weapon.

As Yi Wan faced the other man, he felt the sweat trickling down his spine, and had to will himself to be calm. To think of technique was to fail. The counter-action had to begin instinctively as soon as the attack was launched. Too soon would enable the direction of attack to be changed; too late would mean an accident. A sudden flash of steel, a side-step, an armlock, and the weapon clattered to the ground! Yi Wan let out his breath in a long sigh. He had done it! Now, he had to prove that he had exerted the minimum force necessary, and show that his partner was not hurt.

Master Su had always taught them, 'The lock must be sufficiently painful to deter the aggressor, but when it is released, there must be no pain or injury left.'

It was all right. Yi Wan's partner picked up his weapon with no sign of discomfort, and handed it to Yi Wan. Now it was his turn to attack. He willed his partner to succeed. If the man failed to side step, it would already be too late; Yi Wan would be committed to the thrust. If he faked the attack to give his partner a chance, they would both be failed.

A minute later, it was over. Yi Wan could relax. His partner had disarmed him with the same skill that Yi Wan himself had shown. The worst was over, or so he thought, but the hardest bit of the examination was yet to come. Only Yi Wan and So Yeng had passed the practical tests; they now faced the oral examination.

So Yeng was asked to remain, the candidates who had failed were dismissed, and Yi Wan was asked to wait outside. He sat on the wall in the garden alone, trying to remember all that he knew about Tao-ism, Zen Buddhism, and the principles of training. It was fully an hour before So Yeng came out.

'Come, Yi Wan,' Tai Do beckoned, and it was his turn to sit in the lotus position facing his examiners.

'What do you understand by martial virtue? What is Ch'i?'

Question after question followed, not dealing with the

theories he had memorised, but with practical situations that demanded an immediate response. Yi Wan thought it would never end, but at last Master Su stood up, and this was the signal for them all to arise and bow.

'I will give you a letter of qualification tomorrow,' Master Su said, and they bowed again. The end was as simple as that. A letter from the master would confirm Yi Wan's status anywhere in China.

The next day, when Su gave him this all-important document, he had another surprise for Yi Wan.

'You have been serving me without pay for this last six years,' he said, 'and as some reward, I propose to arrange for you to spend a year at Shaolin, to further advance your martial art studies. Do you know where Shaolin is?'

Yi Wan had heard students speak with awe of this famous centre. It lay in the Hohan mountains to the north, and was the celebrated monastery founded by Tamo, when he had come from India, just over a century before. To go to Shaolin was the dream of every martial arts student in China. It was said that Tamo had invented his system of self-defence primarily as an exercise to fit the monks for the rigorous discipline of their monastic life. Whether this was true or not, their reputation as fighters was fabulous and grew with every traveller's tale.

'Entry is difficult,' Su went on. 'I have spoken with some of the local monks, and have learnt that in a few weeks a small group of them are returning to Shaolin. Few of the lay students who apply to go there are admitted, but the monks feel that as a graduate of my school, the Abbot will probably accept you, but on one condition.'

'What is that?' Yi Wan asked anxiously.

'That you also qualify in medicine. They need a doctor at Shaolin, and if you will practise medicine there, they will teach you more of the martial arts than I ever could.'

Yi Wan could scarce believe this latter statement.

'Am I ready for the acupuncture exam yet?' he asked.

He had been concentrating so much on his Wu Shu

practice that even medicine had taken second place in the
past few weeks.

'You will have time to revise, and I will give you extra
tuition. Forget the Wu Shu for a while; just do your
suppleness exercises. Practise on the doll. I will arrange for
your examination in Po-yang, before the regional board, and
Tai Do and So Yeng will accompany us there. It is never wise
to travel outside the town alone.'

Telling Poppy of his good news and of Master Su's
generosity, Yi Wan had a shock.

'When you return from Shaolin, I may not be here.'

'What do you mean, Poppy?'

'I shall be twenty-one. My bond-service will be over.'

'But where will you go?'

'Home. Perhaps my parents will have arranged a marriage
for me.'

The news ought not to have surprised Yi Wan, but he had
drifted along with no thought of this cloud arising to destroy
their happiness. Foolishly, he had thought that his
relationship with Poppy would last for ever. He had never
allowed himself to think of her as his girl, but had kept their
contact on a formal teacher-pupil level, knowing that this was
correct. To think of touching Poppy, caressing her, or kissing
her, would be unthinkable in this delicately balanced
relationship, and he had never let it enter his mind when they
were together. But when he was alone, he knew that he
wanted a girl, and the girl he wanted was Poppy. This was not
because he did not know any other girls. The one on the
vegetable stall in the market always paid him special attention,
and the one in the leather shop was pretty, but neither of
them compared with Poppy.

He knew, however, that he could not ask any girl to go out
with him, as he might have done in his home village, nor was
he in a position to offer marriage. In any case, marriages were
arranged in this part of the world. It was only in tiny remote
places like his home that young people could sometimes pair
up with the person of their choice.

Now, at the thought of losing Poppy while he was away at Shaolin, Yi Wan felt he was losing part of himself. She suddenly became infinitely precious to him, and he saw that not only did he love her as a sister, but that he also loved and wanted her as a woman.

'Supposing your parents have not arranged a marriage for you, will you come back and work for Master Su?' he asked.

'If he wants me to.'

'I am sure he will, Poppy. I want you to.'

'You?'

'What I am trying to say, Poppy, is that I love you.'

At this, she laughed merrily.

'You cannot say this to me,' she protested. 'I am no-one. I am a servant-girl. Even when my bond-service is over, I am still a servant. You are going to be a doctor, or a teacher of Wu Shu, at least. You will be rising to the Shih class.'

'My parents were of the Nung, the same as your's, Poppy. We are the same as each other, and if we were not, would it make any difference? What are these class distinctions but forms?'

'I would hold you back. I am not educated. You will mix with the nobility.'

'And with ordinary people, if I am a doctor. How could you hold me back, Poppy? You are a natural gentlewoman. You have learnt the ways of polite society in this house. You have learnt to read, which other girls cannot do.'

'Thanks only to you.'

'Don't you love me, Poppy?'

'Of course I do, Yi Wan, but what can I say? What can we do? I must obey my father and mother, and you must go wherever life calls you.'

'I hope to return here and work in Master Su's practice as his assistant.'

'I hope that is possible, but whether you do that or not, you are bound to grow away from me. You will be absorbed in your patients and your students. Like Master Su is.'

'I shall never grow away from you, Poppy. I shall always

want you. Please remember that.'

She promised, but deep in his heart, a cold feeling warned Yi Wan that she might be wiser than he in predicting their future.

Seven

On the road to Po-yang, Master Su and Tai Do rode ahead as befitted elders, and So Yeng and Yi Wan followed at a courteous distance behind them. Yi Wan had not ridden often enough to be at home on a horse, but he managed the animal with reasonable skill, and was able to keep up with the party.

Although he had not previously known So Yeng very well, they had spoken several times since they had both received their qualifications. So Yeng was going to spend a further year at Master Su's school, and then would take up an appointment with the military establishment in his home town, training officers. This was a regional centre some two hundred miles distant.

Their road lay across semi-desert, but was well trodden, and the mountains to the south gave them guidance. Some miles out of the town, Master Su reined in his horse, and pointing to a track that led southwards, he said, 'Poppy's parents live down there.'

'How far?' Yi Wan asked.

'Fourteen miles. I wanted to point it out to So Yeng, because he will probably have to escort her home, when she reaches her majority. She has no brothers to come and fetch her, and her father will be too busy on the farm. And of course she could certainly not travel alone.'

This reminder saddened Yi Wan, and he fell silent for much of the rest of the journey, only rousing himself to answer So Yeng's direct questions.

The town of Po-yang was much bigger than Tunhuang, and they had ample warning that they were approaching from the number of small holdings that clustered around the outskirts. Unlike Tunhuang, which was compact and partly walled in, the provincial capital had suburbs, in which dwellings became more and more numerous.

When they entered the street leading to the main square, there seemed to be people everywhere, women going about their shopping, men cleaning the streets, farmers driving carts of produce or flocks of animals to market, citizens talking in groups, and individuals wandering about with no apparent purpose. Yi Wan had never seen such crowds.

Master Su led the way through the throng, and after passing the market and the mosque, they turned down a side road, and stopped at an inn. Tai Do went inside to make enquiries, and came out very quickly to confirm that rooms were available and that there was stabling for the horses. The inn-keeper himself followed Tai Do, welcoming his guests with a deep bow, and calling on his grooms to take their horses and water them.

When a meal had been prepared and they had eaten, they were shown to rooms on the first floor. Yi Wan found that he was to share an apartment with So Yeng.

'You have been to Po-yang before, haven't you, So Yeng?' Master Su asked.

'Yes, when I was on my way to study at your school.'

'Then show Yi Wan the sights, when you have rested, but do not let him become over-tired. His examination is tomorrow.'

For the next two days, Tai Do and So Yeng were left to their own devices. These were the most important days of Yi Wan's life. On what happened during them, his future career and his chance of going to Shaolin depended.

Master Su accompanied him to the examination hall, and when he had presented his own credentials and vouched for Yi Wan as one of his students, he left Yi Wan there, and the tests began. There were two examiners, both old men, even by comparison with Master Su. They were doctors who had passed the retiring age. Those who could still work were too busy to undertake the examination of candidates for the profession.

Yi Wan knew that the first day's examination would be an oral one. It was based on the Nei Ching, the first and only book on acupuncture then existent. Since Master Su had presented him with a copy, Yi Wan had read it a dozen times. The book dated back to 2697 BC, when Huang Ti, the father of acupuncture had worked out the principles of anatomy and health with his doctor, Ch'i Po.

Master Su was not allowed to be present at his pupil's examination, but he waited in an outside room. He had taken Yi Wan through the book so many times, that he was confident the young man would succeed. Yi Wan wished that he could be as certain. He knew that a single wrong answer in this part of the examination could fail him.

The examiners took it in turn to fire questions at him, not following the logical order of the book, but choosing them at random, so that he had to think carefully before answering. This was to make sure that he understood the principles, and had not simply learnt the answers by rote.

'Name the five elements.'

'Wood, fire, earth, water, metal.'

'What do you understand by the mother-son law?'

'How would you calm Yin or Yang?'

'Where would you insert a needle to enable teeth to be pulled without pain?'

Throughout three hours of questioning, no indication was given as to whether Yi Wan had answered correctly or not. The examiners sat impassive, neither making marks on the papers before them, nor showing any emotion. There was a break at midday for a meal, and Master Su took Yi Wan back to the inn. Yi Wan was almost too nervous to eat, but Su told him to relax.

'You know all the answers, Yi Wan,' he said. 'Just do not let them fluster you.'

Not wishing to tire his pupil by questioning him in the lunch break, Su talked of other things, and Yi Wan went into the afternoon session refreshed. Three more hours of questioning followed, and at the end of the day, the Chief Examiner told him simply, 'We shall see you tomorrow.' They all bowed, and the two old men left the room.

'Does that mean that I have passed?' Yi Wan asked Master Su.

'Yes, as far as today's examination is concerned. If you had failed, they simply would not ask you back.'

Yi Wan felt prostrate with relief.

'Don't try to study this evening,' Master Su advised him. 'Go out with So Yeng again. It is no good trying to cram knowledge into your head at the last minute. If it is not there now, it won't be tomorrow. But I am certain that you know all that is required. I should not have entered you for the examination otherwise.'

Fortified by Su's faith in him, Yi Wan approached the second day with more confidence. This day was devoted to practical tests. As soon as he arrived, he found a doll waiting for him, exactly like the one Pei had brought for him to practise on. It stood in a corner of the room, and a wax coating had already been applied to cover all the holes.

'We are going to give you six cases to consider,' the Chief Examiner told him. 'You may ask whatever questions you consider necessary about the patient, and you must then tell us what is wrong with him and the treatment you propose to give. If we agree with your diagnosis, we shall ask you to demonstrate on the doll exactly where and how you will insert the needles. Have you the various needles to hand?'

'Yes, sir.'

'This is Case Number One. A woman, forty-seven years old. What do you want to know about her?'

'Where was she born?'

'In this town.'

'At what season?'

'Spring.'

'At what time of day is she consulting me?'
'Now.'
'So it is nine o'clock in the morning and early Summer.'
'Yes.'
'Is she married or single?'
'Married.'

So the questioning went on, until Yi Wan was able to identify her probable condition as poisoning, and recommend treatment with the fire needle and moxabustion. This was a technique so rarely used that he was hesitant to suggest it, but as soon as he had made the proposal, he knew that he was right, for the examiner asked for demonstration on the doll.

The confidence that his first success gave him enabled Yi Wan to sail through the other five cases, and the morning session was over. In the afternoon a different kind of test would await him.

Four patients were brought in for this, whose condition was known to the examiners. They were all volunteers. Yi Wan was asked to take their pulses, and to determine by pulse diagnosis alone what was wrong with them, and then to state what treatment he would recommend. He knew that pulse diagnosis was fundamental to the practice of acupuncture. The more highly skilled doctors could tell by this means not only the patient's present condition, but what he was likely to suffer from. Illness showed up in the pulses long before any other symptom could be detected and long before the patient himself complained. Another use of pulse diagnosis was in treating a lady of rank. It was forbidden for a doctor to look on the naked form of such a lady, and the taking of the pulses was therefore his only means of telling what was wrong with her.

Yi Wan remembered his first attempt to take the pulse in Master Su's consulting room. He had found difficulty in feeling even one pulse then. Now he had to find all three superficial ones, and then the three deeper ones, and to detect twenty-seven different qualities in each of them. But he must put past failures behind him. Confidence was half the battle.

His first case badly shook that confidence. Although he found every pulse easily enough, he could detect nothing abnormal in any of them. This indicated that there was nothing wrong with the patient, but he reasoned that there must be. Why else would they bring him in as a test case? What was he missing? The examiners had said he was a patient. Therefore he had to have some condition that Yi Wan was failing to spot. Calming his own pulses, Yi Wan went through the entire routine again. He wanted to question the patient, but he knew that this was forbidden. His diagnosis must be on the pulses alone.

He felt that the examiners were becoming impatient with him, but try as he would, he could find nothing wrong.

'Well?'

The Chief Examiner almost barked the question.

Yi Wan had to answer.

'This patient is perfectly fit, sir.'

With trembling, Yi Wan announced the fact, certain that he had muffed his chances, and that he was about to be failed.

'Of course he is. Why didn't you say so the first time?'

Even the examiners permitted themselves a smile, and Yi Wan knew that the worst was over. He had avoided the trap set for him, and his success gave him the confidence he needed. He sailed through the rest of the examination.

Late in the evening, they presented him with his Diploma, in the presence of Master Su, who was also required to sign it, as Yi Wan's teacher. Yi Wan was now a qualified doctor. Shaolin was his.

Two days later, he did not need to tell Poppy of his success. She knew when he went to her room to give her a reading lesson, and impulsively she threw her arms around him. For the first time, he held her, feeling her firm young body pressed against his in love, and he remembered with a pang of pain that she might soon go out of his life. He wanted to kiss her, and to ask her to wait for him, but he knew that these things simply were not done in the society in which they lived. Custom was custom, and everyone accepted. They could not fight the rules that governed society.

Master Su had something else to tell him, when he went to the consulting room.

'Before the first patient arrives, let me congratulate you on your success.'

'It is all due to your kindness, Master.'

'And your hard work. I told you on the day you came here, Yi Wan, that it was my desire to see that you had an education that would fit you for your place in the world. Now that you have qualified, I can no longer expect you to serve me freely. From now on, I shall employ you as my assistant, at the usual salary. And if you will help with the Wu Shu classes, I will pay you the accepted rate for that as well. I would like you to take the afternoon patients, so that I can use that time to teach the senior pupils weapon techniques. In the morning, when you have finished teaching Poppy to read, I would like you to take the third year students. You will need money when you go to Shaolin, because although they do not use coinage there, you will have expenses on the journey. However, do not worry. I will give you a lump sum when you leave, in recognition of your work over the past six years, and I hope, when your training at Shaolin is finished, that you will come back and assist me here once more.'

'I will, Master,' was all Yi Wan could answer, because he was so full of gratitude, he was near to tears.

He thought afterwards that he wished he could have asked Master Su to speak to Poppy's father on his behalf, but he knew, even as soon as it occurred to him, that this was something even Master Su could not do for him.

Eight

Master Su delayed Yi Wan's departure until he had been in touch with the Abbot and confirmed what the local monks had told him about the likelihood of Yi Wan's admission to Shaolin. This enquiry took a couple of months, since it depended on waiting until someone went to the monastery and returned.

During this waiting period, Yi Wan worked both in the medical practice and in the training hall, but his happiest hours were those in which he gave Poppy reading lessons. For years he had sublimated his sexual feelings in his work, but they troubled him more and more as the days passed. He wanted a woman, and often found himself day-dreaming of making love. He did not relate these dreams to any specific woman, least of all to Poppy, because he knew that if he could not marry her, he would not want to use her body simply to satisfy his carnal desires. She was too good and too precious to him to be even thought about in that way. He found pleasure simply in being in her company, hearing her voice, watching her as she bent over her lessons, enjoying her trust. It was a trust that he would never violate, even in his secret thoughts.

He raged within his soul that custom did not allow him to marry her, but he knew that she was right in what she had told him. They must obey the rules of their society. These brief morning sessions, in which they must always behave as pupil and teacher, were the only contact they could ever enjoy. His feelings were made even more unendurable by the fact that he knew she loved him as much as he loved her. If it would have changed the situation, he would even have renounced going to Shaolin, but their love was hopeless.

Inevitably, in late summer, the day of parting came. For the last time, Yi Wan went to give Poppy a lesson, but he could not waste their last moments together hearing her read.

'They are coming for me in an hour,' he said. 'I want you to know, Poppy, that I shall always think of you. If you are here when I come back, or if your father should not have arranged a marriage for you, or if you are ever unhappy ...'

'Hush,' she said. 'Do not say it, Yi Wan. I know.'

Seeing how near she was to tears, Yi Wan felt himself choked with grief. Gently he held her, not daring to speak, not daring to kiss her. When they did speak again, it was of something quite ordinary.

'Xi Hang is going to take care of your cat,' she told him.

'Yes. She is a good woman.'

'Have you warm clothes for the mountain, Yi Wan?'

'Yes. They are all packed.'

At the last moment, he pressed into her hand, a small packet, containing a brooch which he had bought in the market.

'It is nothing,' he said, when she opened it, and exclaimed in delight, 'just a small keepsake, for you to remember me by.'

Impulsively, she put her arms around him and kissed him. It was a gesture that meant more to him than anything she could have given him. He would treasure that moment for ever.

Three monks were waiting at the door for him. Brother Mo was the eldest and the leader of the party. He was sixty years old, tall and very thin. He was going to Shaolin for the last time. He would not return. With him were Xun and Yang. They were younger men, thin faced, but cheerful of disposition. Indeed, Yi Wan had never found Buddhism to be a religion of long faces and undue solemnity. Each of the brothers was clad in the traditional orange robe, and each carried a heavy pack. Yi Wan shouldered his own load, and fell in behind them. Master Su, his wife, Tai Do, Xi Hang and

Poppy all came into the garden to see him off, and as they trudged down the dusty street out of the town, Yi Wan looked back again and again, until they were completely out of sight. He felt that a chapter of his life had ended, and the sadness in his heart was almost as deep as when he had been torn from his home village seven years before, and his childhood had ended for ever.

For the first day of the journey, they were walking through inhabited country, though the farms became more isolated the farther they went, but by the second day they were in the desert, and the mountains to the south had disappeared in the heat haze that hid the horizon. Here there was nothing but sand and scrub vegetation interspersed with cacti. It was a trackless wasteland, and Brother Mo took his directions from the sun.

Two days into the desert, a sandstorm arose. It began as a cloud on the horizon, which quickly became a rushing wind that tore at their clothes and made it difficult even to stand.

'Cover your face with your cloak,' Mo shouted to Yi Wan. 'It will pass in a few minutes.'

Clutching each other and their staves for support, the four men huddled together, their noses and mouths covered against the thick dust that suddenly swirled around them. It filled the air and blotted out the sun, so that Yi Wan felt he was already buried in sand. He could not breathe, and his shallow gasps of air burnt his throat. He thought that he was choking, and that the air would not get to his lungs in time to sustain him until his next breath. His lungs burned as if they were on fire, and he felt he would collapse if the others were not holding him up. Yet he knew that to lay down risked burial in the dust.

The storm passed as quickly as it had arisen. In a moment the sun came out again, and Yi Wan had never thought its burning rays would be so welcome.

'Camels can sense these storms coming,' Mo told him. 'They become cantankerous. The older ones will snarl and bury their mouths in the sand. Wise men follow their example.

The only way to survive is to cover your nose and mouth. If you don't the sand will get into your lungs and choke you.'

The desert crossing took five days, and reaching the foothills, they began the long climb to the monastery that was their goal. During that time Yi Wan came to appreciate the knowledge and skill of their leader, and ten days into the mountains, he had another demonstration of Shaolin skills.

They were climbing a lonely trail, when they heard sounds of conflict from around a bend in the trail. Dropping their packs, they all ran forward. Two men and a woman were being attacked by brigands. Yi Wan had thought his reactions were fast, but Mo was faster still. He snatched one man off the woman, and threw him over a cliff on the right of the path. Whilst the man's body was still bouncing from rock to rock, he laid out the woman's other assailant with a vicious kick to the throat.

Xun and Yang went to the aid of the two men. One was bleeding from a sword cut, but he fought furiously, regardless of the blood that flowed down his leg. Xun was as swift as Mo had been. Using his staff against swords, he disarmed four of the aggressors in the first seconds, and Yang laid them out with chops to the head and kidneys. The six who remained on their feet, realizing that they were now more evenly matched for numbers and that they were being attacked by monks, fled up the mountain-side, scrambling from rock to rock, losing their weapons in their flight.

Yi Wan helped the woman to her feet.

'Are you hurt?' he asked. 'I am a doctor.'

She was too shocked to answer, but a quick examination told him that she was more shocked than injured, and he turned to the man who had been wounded.

Stemming the flow of blood with pressure on a point in his thigh, Yi Wan asked his companions to fetch cloths to bind the wound. It looked worse than it was.

'Whither are you bound?' Mo asked the travellers.

'To the next village. It is only ten miles up the hill.'

'You were not very wise to set out in such a small group.'

One of the men was about to point out that Mo's party was no bigger, but realizing in time how much more skilful they were at self-defence, he did not utter his thought.

'Where are you going?' he asked instead.

'Shaolin.'

It answered all the man's questions. To a layman, any Shaolin monk had almost supernatural powers.

It was only when they moved on that Yi Wan realized he had taken no part in the fight. His first impulse had been to tend the wounded. He was still stunned by the skill the older brothers had shown. It opened his eyes to the fact that he was still a novice in the field of self-defence, and prepared him to enter his studies at Shaolin with humility, but nothing prepared him for the size and beauty of the monastery, when at last they came upon it.

It was late evening, and the sun tinted the grey walls with a pink glow. Yi Wan could see that it covered several acres, the whole enclosed by an outer wall. Behind the buildings there were trees, but a little higher up the snow line began, and the tops of the hills were ice-bound rock. Already Winter was beginning to set in, and the air was cold.

The main gate of the compound was closed, and along the wall, Yi Wan saw small groups of men who had set up make-shift camps, using brushwood for shelter.

'These are supplicants who ask to be admitted as students,' Mo told him. 'They will stay there all winter for the chance of acceptance.'

Yi Wan had heard of these people. Their persistence in waiting at the gate, enduring the harsh elements, was one of the tests designed to prove their worthiness to enter. He had heard that if they passed this ordeal, and were admitted to the labyrinth of caves under the monastery buildings, they would find other obstacles there, designed to test their determination further.

But for Yi Wan and his party, the gates were immediately opened by a monk who had been posted to watch for their coming. Mo, Xun and Yang were former pupils of Shaolin.

They returned as honoured guests, coming for a period of renewal. And Yi Wan came as a lay doctor and a martial artist of repute.

His travelling companions were at once taken to the main building, which was the hall of meditation, and adjoined the cells where they would sleep. Yi Wan was shown to the Guest House, which was a wing of the Abbot's quarters, and was near the bell tower.

Here he met Wei Zhing, the guest master.

'It is late,' Wei Zhing greeted him. 'Have you eaten?'

'Yes, we had our last meal on the way.'

'Then I will show you at once to your bed, and we will talk in the morning.'

Yi Wan assented, and he was taken to a small bare cell, which contained only a table, a chair, a couch on which to sleep, and washing utensils. There were a few hooks for his clothes, and a shelf for his books and instruments, but the accommodation was as comfortable as his loft had been in Tunhuang, and he had not expected luxury. He was so excited at being here, and so relieved that they had come safely through their journey, that his heart was full of thanks, as he prepared for sleep.

The cell was icy cold when he awoke, and looking through the window, he saw monks shovelling snow to clear the courtyard. He did not know the time, but it was already daylight, and he knew from the many sounds that the monks were all astir.

When he had washed and dressed, the Guest Master joined him, and Yi Wan realized that he slept in the same building and had been waiting for sounds from Yi Wan's room, before disturbing him.

'You had a long journey, and you were tired,' Wei Zhing said pleasantly.

He was a tall rotund man, with a kind face.

'I am sorry I overslept,' Yi Wan told him.

'It is all right. Your breakfast is in the Guests' Dining Hall, and the Abbot will see you later in the morning.'

Walking behind his host down a stone corridor, Yi Wan came to the refectory, where a single place had been set for him at a long table. He took his seat, and immediately a monk brought him a bowl of hot soup and a piece of bread.

'There will be tea in a moment,' the Guest Master said.

Yi Wan was both hungry and cold, and the food and herb tea which followed refreshed him. He stood up and did a few exercises to bring life back to his limbs. If life in the Guest House was as spartan as this, he thought, what must the monks themselves endure.

Following breakfast, Wei Zhing offered to show him around. There were several cell blocks for the monks, and a hall of residence for the lay brothers. Some of these were simply labourers in the Monastery; others were students of Shaolin Temple Boxing. No distinction was made between these groups in their living conditions. There was the great hall of meditation, used by the monks only, the bell tower, the gatehouse, the store-rooms, a library, and a practice hall for the martial arts students. Already, Yi Wan could hear the sounds of bare feet on polished wood and the clack of staff on staff, coming from inside. He longed to be at his own training, but courtesy demanded that he should meet the Abbot first and present his credentials.

Abbot Mian received Yi Wan at midday. He was not an old man, as Yi Wan had expected, but he had an air of great wisdom, and a simple grace. He read Yi Wan's letter of introduction, and looked over his certificates of proficiency in acupuncture.

'Welcome Yi Wan,' he said. 'Wei Zheng will place a room at your disposal for the treatment of the sick. We have a small sick bay for bed patients, and your treatment room will be adjacent. You will live in the Guest House, of course. I understand that you want to study our system of self-defence?'

'If I may,' Yi Wan replied politely.

'Practice for the monks and for the senior students is in the evenings. Only novices train by day. So you can carry out your medical treatments by day, and join the advanced classes in the evenings. If you wish to know more of our faith, that too can be arranged, but there is no compulsion. You are a free man.'

Nine

Yi Wan quickly settled into his duties at the monastery. There was occasional sickness amongst the monks, due to the rigorous nature of their discipline and the harshness of the weather, now that Winter was setting in. None of the monastery buildings were heated, and since stillness and silent meditation was the normal pattern of religious exercise many suffered chills and rheumatic conditions. These could have been much worse had not they all participated in the morning exercises, which maintained good circulation and muscle tone.

Very occasionally, Yi Wan had to treat a patient who had been injured in the martial training, but this was rarer than he had expected when he saw the fierce style of their fighting exercises. Usually the injury was simply a pulled muscle or concussion due to a heavy and awkward fall. Within the practice hall, there was of course the same tradition of taking care of one's partner that Master Su had taught. Much more frequently, he was called upon to treat a pilgrim who had suffered frostbite or accident on the journey to Shaolin, or one of the guests or lay brothers who worked around the monastery.

The room Yi Wan had been given as a surgery was a pleasant one, and faced south, so that it caught the morning sun. The window looked out on a magnificent vista of mountain peaks, which with their covering of snow and the blue backdrop of the sky, gave a feeling of tranquillity that helped to calm patients.

As soon as he was settled, Yi Wan asked to be allowed to join in the morning exercises. Everyone who was not on duty took part. In fine weather, the exercises were held in the main yard of the monastery, and several hundred men would perform them in unison. One of the older monks usually led them, and Yi Wan did not think it was the same one every morning, though in their yellow robes and with their shaven heads, he found it difficult to tell them apart.

Late one afternoon, when he had been there a week, Yi Wan was called to the office of Xun Zi, the chief instructor of fighting techniques. The office was in the main block of the monastery buildings, and was approached by a long corridor that ran down the side of the training hall.

As he came nearer, Yi Wan saw through the open door that the master was seated at a wooden table. He was a short thin man, with shaven head and face, and he wore the traditional jacket and trousers used for practice. He looked up on hearing Yi Wan's footsteps, and smiled in welcome.

With his attention on the master, Yi Wan stepped through the doorway, and immediately his instinct warned him that something was wrong. There was no sound or movement that his senses could have picked up, but continuous practice at Master Su's had developed this faculty of knowing when danger was present and of instantly responding without even thinking.

Two men, hidden by the wall, had been waiting just inside the doorway, and they fell upon Yi Wan with clubs. His immediate evasive turns to left and to right meant that their blows passed him harmlessly by, and catching each by the wrist, he ran forwards, then suddenly doubled back, to bring their bodies together. From here he was able to sweep their legs away and take them both to the ground, where he held them with a wrist lock on each.

He looked up, to meet the master's eye.

'Good,' said Xun Zi. 'You have been well trained. You must forgive the test. For a student's own safety, we need to be absolutely sure he knows what he is doing, before he is admitted to the senior class. You may release those boys. They would not really have harmed you.'

When the two young students had regained their feet, the master dismissed them, and they bowed both to Yi Wan and to Xun Zi, before leaving the office.

'Sit down,' Xun Zi said, motioning to a chair. 'I have your letter of commendation from Master Su, whom I know well. How is he?'

'Well and active when I left Tunhuang,' Yi Wan answered.

'He is now over seventy years old,' Xun Zi said. 'Does he have many pupils these days?'

'About forty seniors and a children's class.'

'He defeated all comers when he was at Changan University,' Xun Zi told Yi Wan. 'He could have become master to the Emperor's body-guard, but he chose to retire to the western provinces. He placed more value on his work as a doctor than on his fighting ability, and he had heard that there was a special need for qualified doctors in Tunhuang.'

'How many train here?' Yi Wan asked.

'There are about sixty seniors in the graduate class, to which you will be admitted. All the monks have some training of course. Lay brothers train in the mornings only.'

'When can I start?'

'Tonight.'

Although free sparring did not form a regular part of training, it was sometimes used to evaluate a student's progress, always without landing any of the blows or kicks, of course, and on his first evening, Yi Wan was matched against two of Xun Zi's men. He realized that he was being assessed, but he was not nervous. The tradition of not injuring a partner was so strictly observed in training halls, that Yi Wan knew he would be taken care of, even if he was hopeless. A graduate could be expelled for treating another student roughly, and expulsion from Shaolin would mean being black-listed by every school in the country. Yi Wan was more concerned that he did not hurt Xun Zi's men, therefore, than that they might hurt him.

He found that each had a different style. The first man depended on high kicks and a fast attacking style. Yi Wan could cope with this by using the fast evasive turns that were a feature of Master Su's school. The second man resorted to grappling, and was able to take Yi Wan to the floor again and again without difficulty, though not to hold him there. Always Yi Wan could twist out of his hold and spring to his feet.

Xun Zi took him aside after these bouts.

'You have clearly learned Master Su's specialty, which is the evasive action,' he said. 'No doubt he told you that his style is based on the willow, which bends with the weight of snow and is not broken, whereas the oak stands firm and is snapped. Or perhaps he reminded you of water, which flows round an object instead of trying to push it aside.'

'Both,' Yi Wan agreed.

'You have learnt to cope with attack very well,' Xun Zi told him, 'but Master Su's is still one of the soft styles. Here at Shaolin we teach a much harder style. Oh, there is room for all that you have learnt, and do not think that I am belittling it, in any way. Don't forget anything that Master Su has told you, because it is of extreme importance to be able to avoid attack, especially if it is made with a weapon. But, when occasion demands, it is also important to have the courage to go in, accepting a blow or a cut, if there is no other way of getting close enough to defeat your attacker. I noticed this morning when we were doing the group exercises that you have mastered abdominal breathing. That is good, as it allows the flow of Ch'i. Deep breathing calms the nerves and takes away fear. Too many fighters are afraid, and their fear forces them into shallow breathing. This only exacerbates their fear. What I should like you to do in your first few weeks of training is to develop strength but without losing your speed, your reflexes, your evasive techniques or your blocks. Later we will teach you the grappling techniques, with which you do not seem so familiar.'

Yi Wan bowed in assent, and the master sent him back into the class.

During the weeks that followed, Xun Zi set him harder and harder exercises to develop his muscles. He had thought he had firm biceps and triceps already, but by the time Xun Zi had been teaching him for three months, he knew that he had been soft. Each day he was set to do a hundred press-ups and a thousand deep knee bends. Xun Zi gave him stones of ever increasing size to lift above his head. At the same time as he was developing strength, he was required to keep his muscles supple by the early morning training. Practice of punches, kicks and blocks was carried out to numbers as in Tai Do's class. Xun Zi was ever watchful, dashing among his pupils to correct a fault, or to show a better technique.

Over the year that followed, Yi Wan gradually learned that the Shaolin system of exercises were all based on the movements of animals. Just as Master Su's techniques grew from observation of the willow tree and of water, so Shaolin techniques had been developed from the observation of animal behaviour.

'We learnt from five creatures,' Xun Zi told him. 'Four of them live in the jungle; the fifth is mythical. They are the snake, from whom we get the grappling movements that you found so unfamiliar. Think of the python coiling around his victim, crushing him, and bearing him down to the ground. Then, the tiger. He has strong fierce attacks, ripping his victim apart with teeth and claws. Your style was too defensive. Learn to move in strongly like the tiger, without fear of consequence. Leap at your opponent as the tiger leaps at the throat of its prey. That is the correct attacking spirit. From the leopard, we learn grace and suppleness. Think how it steals up unnoticed, and then suddenly springs. The leopard's is not the bold face to face attack of the tiger; it is prepared in secret, and sprung swiftly when the victim is least prepared. Yet with all its apparent gentleness the leopard is powerful, and his style is essentially an attacking style, like the tiger's. From the crane, we learn movements that are more akin to your defences. He flaps his wings, in a way that suggests a flurry of arms, beating off attack. He neutralises his opponent's attack first, with this beating of wings. Then he goes in with his powerful beak.'

'And what of the mythical creature?' Yi Wan asked.

'The dragon. He breathes fire. From this legendary beast, we get the idea of the importance of Ch'i, the spirit. You understand something of Ch'i from your acupuncture.'

Shaolin not only taught Yi Wan more about the martial arts than he could ever have imagined; it enabled him to link the philosophy with his medical practice. He was not over-worked in the latter, but he did have a regular daily time of consultations, and he was kept so busy with these two interests that it was not until his year was nearly over that Yi Wan realized his work and studies had driven Poppy from his mind. Regretfully, he wondered if she had been wiser than he, when she had said that he would grow away from her?

He wondered what he would find when he went back to Tunhuang, and almost before he knew it, there remained only his final graduation test between him and, hopefully, his reunion with Poppy.

Ten

The urn used for the graduation test at Shaolin had been pointed out to Yi Wan many times during his stay there. It was made of stone, and was two feet in diameter and three feet high. It stood on a base in the courtyard outside the practice hall, so that pupils could see it every day, as they went in to practice. Empty, it weighed a hundred and eighty pounds.

The test consisted simply in lifting the urn from the base and replacing it in the original position. Students could practice the lift at any time they chose. It was not easy, because it meant wrapping the arms around the vessel and holding it tightly to the chest. The urn was perfectly smooth except for two embossed designs on either side. But, although not easy, it was not too difficult either, Yi Wan thought, until they told him the condition of the test. On the day, it would be filled with burning embers, so that not only a student's strength but his courage, speed and dedication would be tested.

So daunting was the task that many students were content to study at Shaolin without seeking the formal graduation certificate. Simply to have been there for a year gave them standing. The monks themselves did not need to graduate, of course. The martial training was for them secondary to their main purpose, which was the pursuit of religious experience. Having been shown the urn and knowing its purpose, the feat became a challenge. Yi Wan felt that as he had been excused the gruelling initiation ceremonies, he ought at least to satisfy the graduation requirements.

Of all the students this year, only two volunteered to attempt the feat. Yi Wan was one.

On the day, graduates and students all gathered in the courtyard to watch. This was always the most dramatic moment of the student year. Yi Wan had asked to be the first to try, and he stood with the other candidate in front of the assembly. The masters came out with Xun Zi and took their place on the platform, facing the students. Yi Wan took off his shirt, feeling the cool breeze of Autumn on his bare chest and arms. He gained nothing by being the first to make the attempt, because the urn was cooled with water, between each attempt, and a new fire started inside its bowl. He simply felt that he did not want to be present if the other student failed, because the man was a friend of his, nor did he want to see him suffer pain.

Two monks placed the sticks in the urn, and applied a lighted brand. They flared up. They were allowed to burn ten minutes, until the pot was hot. The flames had died down by then, and the residue in the bottom was just red smouldering ashes, but to touch the pot would be like grasping live coals.

Yi Wan had tried to train himself by occasionally touching a hot pot in the kitchen and immediately taking his hand away and dashing cold water over the spot. This prevented blistering if it was done quickly enough, but he knew it was not a real practice for his ordeal today. Then his contact with the pot was momentary. Now, his arms and possibly his body would be in contact with the urn for at least six seconds. That was the shortest time in which he had been able to lift the urn to the required height and replace it correctly. There had also to be a pause at the top of the lift, for the judges to agree that it was high enough. They gave the signal to replace the pot. Yi Wan did not know how long he might have to hold it aloft before they reached their decision.

As he waited, he was conscious of the silent ranks behind him, and he watched the flames leaping from the pot. He tried to calm his mind. He knew that pain was largely in the mind, and it was made worse by anticipation or imagination.

He must think of nothing, achieving the no-mind of Zen. Then, when the moment came, he must count the seconds to take his mind off the agony of burning flesh. No, he must not be dramatic and even think of burning flesh. Students who had passed the test did not suffer lasting injury. They recovered and went on to become famous masters with private schools. The people who set this test were not sadists. They made it difficult but not impossible.

The flames died down, and black smoke arose. The moment was here.

'Now!'

It was not Xun Zi, but his assistant who gave the word.

Yi Wan stepped forward, and mustering all his courage for one mighty effort, he grasped the pot and lifted it clear. Pain such as he had never dreamt of shot through his arms and shoulders. Sweat streamed down his body. he had to bite his lips not to cry out. He felt that consciousness was leaving him, and to control his body, he began to recite in his mind the seconds that were passing. 'One ... two ... three.' Each one seemed an eternity, though he knew how quickly a second usually passed. Would they never give the signal? Had he not held it high enough?

'Down!'

At the word, he crashed it back onto the pedestal, steadying it with his hands, so that it did not topple over and rob him of victory at the last moment. He did not even hear the cheer that went up behind him. He had taken the full weight of the urn on his forearms and his shoulders, but it felt as if the whole of the front of his body had been burnt. He wanted to touch the areas of pain with his hands. He staggered back, unable to focus his gaze on the masters in front of him, or even on the urn itself.

The two monks who looked after the sick bay rushed forward and caught him as he fell. Supporting him, they carried him to the adjacent hall, and laid him on the table they had prepared.

'It's all right. This will soothe.'

The cold compress that they applied seemed to burn as much as the fire, but Yi Wan knew that they were doing the right thing. They were trained to deal with burns. When they had cooled his arms and shoulders and chest, they carried him into the sick bay.

'You will rest here for a few days, master.'

Yi Wan was glad of the darkness of the room, which had only one small opening near the ceiling. He felt that he would never be able to use his arms again, and that it was a ridiculous thing to have attempted. So intent was he upon his own pain that he did not hear the cry of triumph that was raised when the second candidate lifted the urn successfully. He only stirred when the attendants brought in their second patient, and even then he could not speak.

For two days, Yi Wan suffered agonies. He did not want to eat or to talk, but simply to lie quietly and to try and forget what he had done. To think of the test was to experience the pain all over again. He must forget. It was over. He was getting better. On this one thought he must concentrate his mind.

When he could start considering other people again, he realized that the other patient had been lying beside him for two days, and he was full of remorse that he had not spoken to him. Now he asked how the man felt.

'Like you,' was the answer. 'But the burns heal within two weeks. We are not permanently injured, but we are scarred for life.'

'What salve did the monks put on the burns?' Yi Wan asked, his professional interest aroused.

'They use raw potato to cool the wound at first,' the man answered. 'It lessens the blistering.'

The day before they were allowed out of the sick bay, Xun Zi visited them with three of his senior masters.

'Here are your certificates,' he said, unrolling two scrolls, 'though you will not need them to prove you have been to Shaolin.'

Looking at the marks on his fellow patient, and then at his

own arms and shoulders, Yi Wan saw exactly what the master meant. The embossed markings on the urn had branded them both for ever.

'Your two companions are ready to return to Tunhuang, as soon as you are fit to travel,' Xun Zi told Yi Wan, and a week later they set out. Brother Mo was not with them. He had always planned to remain in the mother house of his order.

Their journey back, through a mild Autumn, was much more pleasant than their journey to Shaolin, and it passed without incident.

When they arrived at Tunhuang, Yi Wan's first duty was to pay his respects to his Master. He found Su had aged indefinably, while he had been away. He was still tall and upright, and his skin still had the unlined glow of youth, but the sparkle had gone out of his eyes. Yi Wan remembered that Xun Zi had told him that Su was in his mid-seventies, but this was not a great age. Many masters lived to over eighty.

Su received him in the living room of the house, and Madame Su was also present. This, to Yi Wan, was the final proof that he was being treated as an equal, and no longer as the orphan Su had taken in. He was not a servant now; he was a doctor and a teacher.

'How did you get on?' Su asked, embracing him.

'Shaolin was a wonderful experience,' Yi Wan answered. 'I cannot thank you enough for making it possible for me to go, and indeed for all the other things you have done for me.'

Su's face brightened.

'Welcome back,' he said. 'You will be able to teach me now.'

'There is little that I could teach you, Master,' Yi Wan replied humbly. 'They have a harder style of fighting at Shaolin, but the basic principles you showed me are still valid. Xun Zi, the chief instructor, said that I must never forget them, and they will always form the basis of my system.'

'We have prepared a room for you in the house,' Su said. 'Wu will take you there now, and when you have rested and refreshed yourself, perhaps you will join us for supper.'

There was so much that Yi Wan wanted to ask. How is

everyone? Is Tai Do still here? Is Xi Hang still cooking for you? How is my cat? But, most of all, how is Poppy?

His heart was full of joy that in a few moments he would see her again, because it was part of her duty to serve supper to the family. Yi Wan felt, however, that he did not want her to serve him, since this would accentuate the difference between them. He wanted to be her equal, not placed on a level with her masters. He could not refuse the invitation to eat with the family, however, nor insist on sleeping in his old quarters in the loft. To do either would be an unforgivable discourtesy, and he owed Su everything.

Wu showed him to a comfortable room on the first floor of the house.

'This used to be Pei's,' she said. 'Now it is your's.'

'Until Pei returns.'

'Pei will not come back.'

There was something so final in her statement that Yi Wan wanted to ask why, but a glance at her face told him that his question would be unwelcome, and he left it unspoken.

'Come down as soon as you have washed and changed,' Wu told him.

Left alone, Yi Wan compared the comfort of this room with the bare necessities of the loft where he had lived for so many years. Here, he had a proper bed, an armchair, cupboards for his clothes, shelves for his books, a table, a writing desk, a rich red carpet and thick curtains that shut out all draught. This was a rich man's room, luxurious beyond his dreams. He did not waste too much time in examining it, however, as he did not want to keep his host waiting.

Master Su and his wife were seated at the table, when he went into the dining room, and Su indicated the place set for him on the right of Mistress Wu. When Yi Wan was seated, Su clapped his hands once.

To Yi Wan's surprise, it was not Poppy who appeared in answer, but Xi Hang.

'Yi Wan is back,' Su told her with a smile, and when she had set down the dishes she was carrying, Xi Hang embraced him.

'Welcome,' she said, simply.

'Tell him how his cat is,' Su said. 'He is dying to know, but he hesitates to ask.'

'He is older, of course, but in good health. He terrorises all the other Toms in the district, and he chases all the females. He has probably got several hundred grandchildren by now.'

Yi Wan smiled.

'And where is Poppy?' he wanted to ask, but he had no chance to do so until the meal was over. Master Su would think it odd to enquire after a servant girl, when Yi Wan already knew that she might be gone by the time he returned.

It was Tai Do, who told him the facts, when they met in the garden, later that evening.

'Poppy was sent away. Four months ago.'

'Was her time up then? She had the best part of a year to serve, I thought. I hoped that she would still be here when I got back.'

'She was with child,' Tai Do said.

'How? She was not married, was she?'

'Pei,' Tai Do answered simply.

'But isn't he in Changan?'

'He came on leave. He had failed his exam for the civil service. He hoped to settle here and to find a teaching post in his father's school. Although Master Su had taken away his grade when he was first banished to Changan, he hoped he would be forgiven and that his qualification would have been restored, since his fault was part of youth's follies. Master Su might have found him a post teaching the juniors, because Madame Su would have wanted it, but not after what Pei did to Poppy. That was the end as far as the Master is concerned. Pei has been banished for ever.'

'Where has he gone now?' Yi Wan demanded.

The anger that flared up in his heart was such that he felt he could have sought out Pei that very evening and cheerfully have killed him.

'He returned to Changan,' Tai Do said. 'There was nowhere else for him to go. He has friends or associates there.'

'And Poppy?'

Yi Wan could hardly bear to ask.

'She went home to her father's farm. Master Su excused her the last few months service that was due to him.'

Yi Wan understood now the hardness in Wu Su's face when he had asked her about Pei, and the change in Master Su himself. They had hoped so much for their son. First that he would take over the school here; then, when that plan failed, that he would enter the civil service, a career that could lead to the very top position in the country, under the new Emperor. More than this, they had hoped that he would be an honourable man. Both in his worldly career and in his character, he had failed them. To have taken advantage of a servant girl under their own roof was an act so far below the standard of behaviour demanded of one of their class that it would have disgraced their very name. It would have seemed even worse to Master Su that a graduate in the martial arts should behave in this way. The highest moral code was required of a teacher.

And what of Poppy, now, Yi Wan asked himself? Had she already borne the child? Or was it not due yet? When had Pei been at home? Was Poppy married? Would the husband her father had in mind accept Poppy and her child? Or was there still hope for him? Yi Wan knew that he had to find out.

He told Master Su what he intended to do, the next morning.

'Master, I have heard about Poppy. I must see her. Will you tell me if she is at home, and her address?'

'If you must go, So Yeng shall ride with you,' Su answered. 'It is far too dangerous to travel alone. But, Yi Wan, do not give Poppy your heart. She is like the kitten. She has her own life. She will never be your's. And, don't you see, Yi Wan, that if she were, you could not live here? I need you, Yi Wan. I have longed for your return. Without Pei, there is no-one but you to carry on my work.'

Eleven

So Yeng would have been Yi Wan's own choice of companion for the journey, and he was grateful that Master Su had chosen him.

'Do not hope too much, Yi Wan,' he said, as they were saddling their horses, to set out for the farm. 'Poppy will obey her father.'

'But her father may accept me as a suitor,' Yi Wan protested.

So Yeng was silent, knowing this to be most unlikely.

'Tell me about Shaolin,' he said, changing the subject.

When they turned south from the main road, they followed a dusty trail to a small village, and beyond that to isolated farms. The soil looked richer than that in the northern province where his father had farmed, but Yi Wan knew, from Poppy's father's experience, that drought could still ruin a farmer's chances.

The Quin farm was the farthest from the main road, and as they were coming up to it, Yi Wan realized that he had not even known the family name until yesterday. Poppy had simply been Poppy. He saw that the main crop was maize, but there were also a few scrawny cows, and a herd of sheep on the hill.

As they approached the farm, chickens fluttered and clucked, and a woman came out to see what had disturbed them.

'Madame Quin?' Yi Wan enquired politely.

'Yes, Master, but if it's about the taxes ...'

'We are not from the Provincial Governor's office,' Yi Wan assured her. 'We are from Master Su's. Is your husband at home?'

'No, he is in the fields.'

The woman gestured in the general direction of the hills.

'And your daughter, Poppy?'

'What do you want with her? Hasn't there been enough trouble already?'

'I would rectify the trouble.'

The woman snorted.

'You must speak to my husband,' she said, and returning to the house, she left them. Her abrupt dismissal after her polite welcome showed Yi Wan more clearly than anything else what she thought of anyone from Master Su's household, and he turned enquiringly to So Yeng.

So Yeng shrugged his shoulders, and indicated the path that led to the fields behind the house. Yi Wan mounted and they rode on.

As soon as they had breasted a small hill, Yi Wan saw a man ploughing with a bullock, and he guessed that this was Poppy's father. Coming to the area of ground that he was turning, they again dismounted and waited for him to finish the furrow.

'What can I do for you, Masters?' the farmer asked.

Yi Wan noticed that again they were given the courteous title, and he realized that now his clothes and the fact that they came on horses marked them out as being of a different class from the farmer. Even so would his father have greeted a visiting landlord.

'We are from Master Su's household,' Yi Wan said again. 'I have just returned from being away, and have learned about your daughter, Poppy. I used to teach her reading while she was at Master Su's. She may have told you about me. I wonder if I might speak with her.'

'She wants nothing to do with your sort,' the farmer replied hostilely. 'Haven't you done enough to her?'

'It was not I,' Yi Wan replied, reasonably. 'I have been absent for over a year. I am concerned about Poppy.'

'You need not be. She is well enough at home. We can take care of her.'

'But I am very fond of her,' Yi Wan said, and realizing how totally inadequate these words were to express his real feelings, he added bluntly, 'I love her.'

'Then it is a pity you were not present to give her protection when she needed it.'

Yi Wan was so much in agreement with the farmer that he had no answer to this criticism.

'I would marry her now, if you will give your permission,' he said.

Her father rejected the idea.

'And who are you, Master? Who are your parents? Why have they not made proper approaches? It is unseemly that a young man simply rides up and asks for the hand of my daughter. In any case you are already too late. Arrangements have been made since she was a child. She is betrothed to my neighbour's son, Gao, and in spite of her present condition, he has not withdrawn from the contract. She will marry Gao before the end of the year.'

'And is this her wish?'

'What else? She is a dutiful daughter.'

'May I not speak with her?'

'To what purpose? It is all planned.'

'Simply to wish her well, as an old friend.'

'If that is all,' the farmer conceded suspiciously, 'then, you will find her watching the goats. Yonder with her sisters.'

The girls were seated in a group, under the scant shade provided by a miserable tree. They were half a mile distant. Yi Wan thanked the farmer, and rode forward.

'I will wait for you here,' So Yeng said, before they reached the herd of goats, and Yi Wan rode on alone, grateful for his companion's tact.

He recognized Poppy at once. She was smaller than her sisters, though they were younger than she was. He noticed with sadness that her pregnancy already showed, and felt again a wild anger at Pei.

Not wishing to alarm the goats and force the girls to round them up again, Yi Wan walked the last few hundred yards, leading his horse.

Poppy recognized him at once.

'Yi Wan,' she said.

'Yes. It is I.'

'These are my sisters.'

To cover her confusion, Poppy performed the introductions. Yi Wan bowed to each in turn.

'I must talk with you, Poppy,' he said.

'Tether your horse, and we will walk a little way,' she answered, 'but not out of sight of my sisters, or father will be angry.'

'Tell me what happened,' Yi Wan said, when they were out of the hearing of the others.

'Pei had always been after me, even when I was a little girl,' she said.

'And the day you showed me your bruised arm, he had been making advances to you?'

'Yes.'

'Why didn't you tell me? Yes, I know you thought I would have challenged him to a fight and been killed. But you could have told Master Su.'

'He was always so kind, and he was sad enough about Pei already. You know he was in trouble before he was sent to Changan. That is why he was sent away. They hoped he would study seriously for a place in the civil service, but he was always lazy.'

'Yet he had qualified in the martial arts. That must have taken dedication.'

'He was interested in that. He was a bully. When he was sixteen, he fought a boy in the town and hurt him badly. For this, Master Su stripped him of his grade, and sent him away.'

'Yet when he came home, they still received him.'

'He was still their son.'

'How often did he interfere with you?'

It tortured Yi Wan to ask, but if he did not know, his

imagination would paint an even worse picture than the reality.

'Most times. I was a bond-servant, Yi Wan. In some households, the Master as well as the son, believes he has a right over a servant. I was fortunate that Master Su himself is a man of honour.'

Yi Wan was shocked at this revelation of how a girl could be regarded and treated in their society.

'Pei did not make love to me before this time,' Poppy assured him. 'He only fondled me, and forced me to kiss him. He was more violent the last time he came, however. His father was angry with him because he had failed his exams. Pei wanted a job in the martial arts school, and Master Su thought he was still unworthy. Pei was drunk the night he forced himself upon me. He did not know what he was doing.'

Yi Wan wanted to protest, but rather than waste a moment of their time in arguing, he said, 'I still love you, Poppy. I still want to marry you.'

'But I am already engaged, and Gao has been so kind and understanding. He could have rejected me, because I am bearing another man's child, but he has not done so. I cannot let him down. I cannot bring further disgrace on my family.'

'But don't you love me, Poppy?'

'You know I do, Yi Wan, but what has love to do with me or with anyone in my position? I must obey. I must be thankful that Gao is so forgiving.'

With a deadness in his heart, Yi Wan knew that the moment had come to say goodbye. Poppy was as much a slave to the system as she had been to Su's family. He must not make the parting harder for her. To help her through the next few moments would be the last kindness he could ever show her.

'I hope you will be happy, my dearest,' he said gently. 'Please remember that if your marriage should fall through, or if at any time I can help you, you have only to send for me, and wherever I am, I will come.'

'I know, Yi Wan, but you must not bind yourself so. I will not be unhappy. Only the thought of your unhappiness could make me that. You and I were not meant for each other. I would always hold you back. You must find some girl who will bring you joy, and bear you children, and if you think of me, you must be glad for me.'

There was nothing more to say. Yi Wan was afraid that if he stayed longer, he would beg her to change her mind, and because this was impossible, she would suffer more. He took her two hands in his, and looking for what must be the last time into her eyes, he tried to print every detail of her face into his memory.

'Well, goodbye then,' he whispered. 'I will never forget you.'

'Nor I you.'

He scarce caught her words. Tears blinded him as he turned away, striding to where So Yeng waited with the horses.

The young man did not ask what had been said. He had known from the beginning that Yi Wan's quest was hopeless. In silence they mounted and rode away. Yi Wan could not trust himself to look back, and not until they reached the main road could he trust himself to speak. Then he asked So Yeng his plans, and learnt that the young man already had a career as a teacher mapped out for him in his home town.

Back at Tunhuang, Yi Wan thanked So Yeng, and went into the house. Every corner seemed full of Poppy. He went first to the kitchen, answering Xi Hang's greeting and her call that dinner would be ready in half an hour, but unable to feel any interest in eating. He was thinking that Poppy had lived here, just behind the store room, and that there he had taught her, each morning for six years. There, he had once held her in his arms, and kissed her. Once.

These were the stairs she had climbed so often. This room that he occupied was where Pei ... Stop! In such thoughts lay madness.

Yi Wan sank down on his bed, burying his head in his

hands. Tears of anger and bitterness blinded him. He loved
Poppy as he had never thought he could love a human being.
After what had happened to his parents, he thought he hated
the whole human race, and that all his love was for the helpless,
the kitten he had rescued, the sick who came to him. He
respected Master Su, Xi Hang, and Tai Do, of course, but he
had not loved them. Only the kitten had claimed his love, and
now Poppy.

He knew before he changed his clothes to go down for the
meal that he would have to leave Tunhuang. It was impossible
to remain in this house or even in this town, because everywhere he went, he would see Poppy, and remember that they
had once been here together. Yet, how could he tell Master Su,
who was now old, and depending on him to take over the
medical practice and the school? Yi Wan felt that he was letting
down the one person in the world who had a call upon his
loyalty, but he saw no other answer and no other way.

Master Su did not need to ask what Poppy's answer had
been. Like So Yeng, he had never doubted the outcome of Yi
Wan's journey. Nor was he surprised when Yi Wan told him his
decision to leave Tunhuang.

'Where will you go?' he asked.

'Anywhere as long as it is far away. Anywhere where I can
forget.'

'You will never forget,' Su advised him. 'Nor should you try.
You knew happiness, but happiness and sorrow both pass
away. In time you will accept. What has been can never be
taken away from you, from either of you. Remember the hours
of your life that you shared with Poppy. Remember the
knowledge that you gave her, and that is still part of her.
Remember the joy she gave you. These memories are your's
and her's, experiences you have shared with her and no other.
They will always be part of both of you.'

Yi Wan wanted to believe what Master Su was saying. He
wanted to believe that joy was outside time, that every
experience and every moment he had spent with Poppy was
eternal, forever his and her's.

'If you must go,' Su was saying, 'your best chance of a successful career would be in Changan. I can give you an introduction to a friend of mine there, who has a large acupuncture practice. He may be able to take you on as an assistant, until you can build up your own practice.'

Once again, regardless of his own disappointment and the difficulties that Yi Wan's decision made for him, Master Su was thinking how he could help. It was the way of a Master.

Part 2
CHANGAN

Twelve

Yi Wan sat on a dais at the end of the long practice hall, watching a hundred students being put through their exercises by Hi Peng, his chief assistant. It had taken two years to build up the Tiger Academy of Wu Shu, and he owed a lot to Hi Peng, who was a graduate of a school near Yi Wan's home town in the northern Hopei region. Hi Peng was much shorter than Yi Wan, but he had the same slim build, and his movements in the practice hall were a joy to watch.

Yi Wan had met him soon after his arrival in Changan. Master Su's introduction had ensured that Yi Wan found immediate employment with Wen Di, in his acupuncture practice, and he had found suitable lodgings nearby, but setting up a martial arts school had proved more difficult. A large airy room was necessary, and such rooms were not easy to find at a rent he could afford. It was Hi Peng who had come to the rescue. His father owned a silk factory, and he allowed them to set up their school in the loft above the packing department.

When the preliminary exercises were over, Yi Wan left the dais, and stepped down onto the floor of the hall. The students immediately fell back respectfully, waiting around the edge to watch the master's demonstration.

'Attack, block, and counter attack,' Yi Wan said, and calling Hi Peng forward, he bowed to him, before demonstrating.

Easily and slowly, he showed each separate element of the movements, then speeded them up until they were one.

'Take partners. Slowly at first; then speed up.'

As the students practised, Yi Wan and Hi Peng moved amongst them, correcting faults, commending accuracy.

'Now, the flying kick.'

So it went on, demonstration and practice, until the lesson was over. When the students had been dismissed, Yi Wan and Hi Peng had their own practice to do. This was essential for all masters, if they were to keep up their own skill. For the next hour, they worked through the eighty-three movements that comprised Yi Wan's system. It was a mixture of Master Su's teaching and Shaolin, modified with some of Hi Peng's ideas.

'Come for a meal,' Hi Peng suggested, when they had finished and washed and dressed.

Yi Wan assented, and they descended an outdoor staircase, crossed the factory yard, and came into a narrow alleyway that led to the main street. Their academy was in the business sector of the town. Across the river was the Palace of the Emperor, the government buildings, the homes of aristocrats and higher civil servants. Down by the river bank were the homes of the poor. But here, in the commercial centre were shops and factories. Most traders lived above their shops.

Hi Peng led the way to the Turkish restaurant, where they usually ate. It was famous for its kebabs.

When they had ordered, Hi Peng said, 'Tell me, Yi Wan, why did you refuse to accept that Army officer as a pupil this morning?'

Yi Wan did not resent the question. Since Hi Peng was a partner in the school, he had a right to know.

'I decided long ago that I would never teach the military,' he answered.

He had never told Hi Peng the story of his life, other than mentioning that they came from the same region of China. Hi Peng knew nothing of the War, because his father had left the north to seek his fortune in the city, long before the conflict with Korea.

'I may be prejudiced,' Yi Wan continued, 'but I find that I cannot relate to the military, and there must be a certain rapport between master and pupil. The cause is past history, but the feeling is still there inside me. Soldiers killed my parents.'

'Our own men?'

'Yes, when driven back in defeat, they started to pillage villages, confiscating grain, robbing ordinary people. Our elders pleaded with them, but they were immediately executed. Villagers and farmers tried to intervene, but it was scythes against swords, stones against crossbows, untrained men against the army. Our men and women were hacked down; our homes looted and set on fire.'

'How did you escape?'

'Our farm was outside the village, and my father made me hide there when he went to the soldiers, hoping reason would prevail, and that they would listen to the elders. I crept out and followed him. I saw everything that happened. They ran a spear through my mother, when she tried to come between an officer and my father. A neighbour made me go back to the house, or I would have fought them too. I hid in an outhouse, while they burnt our home. They found me, and one was going to kill me at once. I wish he had, but another stopped him. I did not know why, but it seems I would have value, if sold to a trader from the west. So they took me to Changan, and sold me into slavery.'

'Obviously you escaped.'

'Yes. Once we were away from the city, and following the Silk Road, the man who had bought me loosened my bonds, so that I could walk beside the camels, and did not have to be carried on the front of his saddle. He reasoned that I was a docile boy and that it was unlikely I would be so foolish as to run off in the desert. But I was beginning to learn what fate awaited me in Persia. I was lucky. I took my opportunity just before we came to the Taklamakan desert. When the camel train had moved forward, I found my way to the town of Tunhuang. There I was taken into the home of Master Su, of whom I have spoken to you. To him I owe everything.'

Hi Peng wanted to ask, if this were so, why Yi Wan had left

Master Su, but something in his companion's manner told him that this would be an unwelcome question. They had not had such an intimate conversation before, in all the months they had been together.

'I too have no love of soldiers,' Hi Peng said suddenly. 'They killed my brother.'

'I am sorry,' Yi Wan answered. 'Do you want to tell me?'

'Wei joined up as a volunteer,' Hi Peng said, launching into his tale with a readiness that told Yi Wan he would find it helpful to talk about the matter.

'As you know, our Emperor has abolished conscription, and he has set up a small peace-time Army of volunteers. I can assure you that the Army is disciplined now and that they are not like the conscripts and mercenaries who raided your village. It was discipline that led to my brother's death. It is harsh in the extreme, but it works.'

'What happened?'

'My brother's platoon was out on manoeuvres. One or more of the soldiers robbed a farmer and raped his wife and daughter. I am sure my brother was not involved. He was a man of honour and would never have done such a thing. His sole purpose in joining the Army was to serve the Emperor.'

'Then why was he punished?'

'You don't know how discipline is applied. If the soldiers responsible for a crime will not own up, the whole Platoon is punished. In this case, they were lined up on the square. The Commandant gave the culprits a last chance to speak out and accept their just punishment with honour. Knowing that punishment for their crime would be death, they kept quiet. The Commandant had no option but to give the order. Every tenth man in every tenth row was called out. They were executed instead. My brother was one of them.'

'The innocent for the guilty?'

Yi Wan could not find words to express his horror at the injustice.

'The Commander had no choice,' Hi Peng said. 'If he had not obeyed the rules, he would have faced the punishment.'

This ethic of unquestioning obedience troubled Yi Wan, because he saw that it was this that had lost him Poppy, but he had to accept that he could not change society.

It was in a mood made sombre by memories that they left the restaurant and walked to Hi Peng's father's house, which was in a street not far from the factory. When he left his friend, Yi Wan proceeded to his own lodging, but tonight he took the long way round. He was restless, and knew he would not sleep until he had worked off his energy and his anger with exercise.

What he really wanted was a woman. He had been conscious of this need, more and more, since coming to Changan. In the first year, getting established in his medical work and setting up his school had absorbed his energies, but now sexual desires surfaced more often, demanding fulfilment.

He saw the girl before she saw him. She was crying in a doorway. He would have asked if he could help, but realizing he was there, she quickly dried her tears and linked her arm in his.

'You want a good time?' she asked. 'You come with Suzie?'

She looked too unhappy to give anyone a good time, but she was young and good-looking, and he felt her breasts pressed against him, as she put her arms round his neck.

'Come,' he said.

His apartment near the factory had its own private entrance and Yi Wan knew they would not be disturbed. The girl looked around the room, seeing the single bed against the wall, the wash basin, the row of books and bottles on the shelf.

'You are a scholar,' she said, calculating if this also made him rich.

Yi Wan neither assented nor disagreed.

'First, you have a little present for Suzie?'

This was a turn-off for Yi Wan. He had wanted her before, but realizing it was so blatantly a commercial transaction for her, his need evaporated. But he knew that he had invited her here, and because he had taken up her time, justice demanded that she be paid. He felt in his pocket, and found a silver coin. The girl slipped it into the shabby bag she carried, and Yi Wan knew at once that he had given her too much.

Pressing herself against him, she put her arms round his neck, and pulled his head down for a kiss. Through their clothes, Yi Wan could feel her breasts. He felt his desire rising again. The girl sensed this, and placed her hand on his genitals.

'I want you,' she pretended.

Yi Wan already had a firm erection.

Quickly, they stripped, and as he took her to the bed, the last of his scruples vanished. His only fear was that he would ejaculate too soon and lose the full pleasure.

Then he saw the bruises on her thighs, and his desire vanished at once.

'Who did that?' he asked, angrily.

'A man. But what does it matter? It's nothing to you. come on.'

But already, Yi Wan knew that he did not want to.

'I am a doctor,' he said. 'I can give you something to soothe the pain of those bruises. Was that why you were crying?'

'Well, you're a queer one,' the girl responded. 'You bring me here, and now you don't want me.'

'I've paid you,' Yi Wan pointed out. 'You haven't lost anything. And I am offering to help you.'

'And I think you mean it,' the girl said, with wonder.

Yi Wan was already searching in his cabinet for a salve.

'Take a night off,' he said, when he had applied it. 'Go home and rest.'

The girl laughed mirthlessly.

'And lose money? I'd get worse than these if I did that.'

'Who would harm you so?'

'My employer.'

'What do you normally earn in a night?'

'Ten coins like you gave me.'

Yi Wan counted them out.

'Have you a home?'

The girl shook her head.

'Only my employer's house.'

'Then stay here till morning. I will not touch you.'

Suddenly realizing that he was naked, he began to pull on his underclothes.

'You may have the bed,' he said. 'I will be comfortable on the couch.'

He turned out the lights.

In the early morning, the girl's movements awakened him.

'I must go now,' she said. 'Even when I spend a night with a client, my employer expects me back for breakfast.'

'Take this bottle,' Yi Wan said. 'Apply the ointment to your bruises twice a day. If they don't get better, come to my surgery. It is at Number three, Goyuko Street.'

Suddenly the girl kissed him, really and with love.

'Thank you,' she said, and the next moment she had gone.

Thirteen

Yi Wan did not see the girl again, and on the anniversary of the establishment of the Wu Shu academy, Hi Peng issued an invitation.

'My honourable father would deem it a pleasure if you would come to dinner with us.'

'The pleasure would be mine,' Yi Wan answered.

He had few social contacts, and although he had met Hi Peng's father at the latter's office, he had never been to their home.

They lived in a substantial house not far from the silk factory, and were clearly merchants of the Shang class, though class distinctions were now becoming blurred in China.

The house reminded Yi Wan of Master Su's, but there was only a very small stone garden at the back, laid out after the Zen pattern, and there were no stables. The living room in which he was received was comfortable, however, with upholstered chairs, a couch, an Indian carpet, and curtains of the finest silk. Madame Peng was a small frail-looking woman with white hair and tiny gentle hands. Master Peng was also of short stature, but he was robustly built, and had the keen look and swift movements of a man who knew what he was about. Yi Wan knew that he must be a good businessman to make his factory pay when there was so much competition.

When introductions had been completed, Madame Peng said to Hi Peng, 'Call your sister, and we will go into the dining room. I am sure Yi Wan is ready to eat.'

Yi Wan had not known that Hi Peng had a sister, or even a brother until he had heard the story of the latter's death. He wondered how many others there were in the family. It was only the one girl who followed them into the dining room, however, and before they took their seats at the table, Hi Peng introduced her.

'This is Yi Wan. This is Jainu.'

Yi Wan turned and saw a slight wisp of a girl, dressed in the current fashion of a long gown with wide sleeves. Her hair had streaks of grey, and he immediately thought that she must be older than Hi Peng, but when she smiled, her face took on a quite different and more youthful appearance, so that Yi Wan found it difficult to place her in the family.

He bowed, and she inclined her head in acknowledgement.

'Sit here,' Madame Peng said, indicating a place on the right of Master Peng. She herself took the seat at the foot of the table, and Hi Peng and Jainu sat opposite each other. Master Peng rang a small hand-bell, and a maid brought in the first course. It was birds' nest soup.

Master Peng enquired politely how the school was making out. He already knew from his son that it was very prosperous, and his question was asked more out of courtesy than from a desire to extract information from his guest. Yi Wan answered, and in his turn asked about the silk business. These politenesses over, Master Peng began to ask about Yi Wan's life in the north, and Yi Wan told him the sad story of his parents' death.

'We came from a small town, not thirty miles from where you lived,' Master Peng said. 'But we had left, ten years before the War. You would have been three years old. Hi was only nine and Jainu was seven. Little Wei was only two.'

'Were you in the silk industry when you lived in Hopei?' Yi Wan asked.

'No. I was apprenticed to a blacksmith. We made farm implements. My uncle founded the factory here in Changan, and as he had no sons to carry it on, when he died, he left it to me. It was quite a small family business then, but now we employ over two hundred girls.'

His success was clear from the life style of his family. Yi Wan took note of all that he was saying, but in his mind he was calculating that Jainu was only four years older than he was. He had been mistaken in thinking she was older than Hi Peng. She was very quiet during the meal, and Yi Wan wondered if she was normally as subdued as this, or whether she was simply shy in the presence of a guest.

The soup was followed by a beef dish served with rice and almonds, and they went on to lychees, and wine. There appeared to be two servants, who took it in turns to bring in the dishes.

After they had eaten, Master Peng suggested that they should adjourn to the sitting room, and Jainu and her mother excused themselves and left the men to their own devices.

'Do you play Go?' Master Peng asked.

'I have not done so,' Yi Wan answered.

'Then shall I teach you?'

When Yi Wan assented, he got out the board and tiles.

The game was not difficult to learn, and once Yi Wan had picked up the idea, he was surprisingly proficient. They played for three hours, and did not notice how time was passing.

'You must forgive me,' Yi Wan said at last. 'I have kept you from your bed.'

'Not at all,' Master Peng assured him. 'I have not enjoyed an evening so much for months. My family won't play with me because I beat them. You must come again. Anytime.'

After the visit, Yi Wan found himself thinking increasingly not of her father and their game, but of Jainu. He wondered if she was married, or if a contract had been made for her marriage. He knew this was the custom with rich merchants, and Jainu was so attractive that he could not imagine her parents having any difficulty.

This did not stop Yi Wan from being attracted to her, and dreaming about her. He had to face facts. He wanted a woman. He was disgusted that he had nearly found release of his desires with a prostitute. Sex was an expression of love between people who cared for each other. He needed a wife, and since Poppy could never be his, it was time he took steps to find one.

A certain delicacy of feeling prevented him from asking outright whether Jainu was engaged or not, but he saw her every time he went to Master Peng's house, and he found himself growing fond of her. Soon, he was making a point of going every Saturday evening, and he had to admit to himself that it was not the games of Go with Master Peng that were the attraction. It was the hope of talking to Jainu.

When he admitted his fondness to himself, he knew that he must ask Hi Peng the situation.

'Jainu was engaged to be married,' Hi Peng told him. 'But the boy died, six months ago. He was a clerk in my father's office, and he was fetching the wages from the bank, when he was set upon by an armed gang. They robbed him and when he tried to pursue them, they cut his throat. He was a good man, the son of one of our neighbours, and he would not always have been a clerk, of course. He was working through all the departments of my father's business, so that he would learn it from top to bottom, and when father retires, it was hoped he would take over as manager.'

'I am sorry,' was all Yi Wan could say. 'Will you go into the business now?'

'No. I am a teacher of Wu Shu. That is my choice of profession. Father accepts that.'

'I am fond of your sister,' Yi Wan confessed. 'Tell me, Hi Peng, is there any chance for me?'

'For myself, I would be most honoured if you married into our family,' Hi Peng answered. 'My father, too, would most certainly welcome you. He finds you a most agreeable companion, despite the difference in your ages. Mother would accept whatever father decrees.'

'And Jainu?'

'You would have to ask her.'

'What should I do?' Yi Wan pursued. 'What is the

procedure? I know that marriages are arranged in your class. At home, we might just speak to a girl, but I see that this would not be proper in this case.'

'Speak to father,' Hi Peng said.

Yi Wan was nervous about making this approach. He was acutely conscious that he was not of the merchant class but one of the peasantry. He wondered if it would be thought that he was taking advantage of the kindness shown him by the open invitation to the Peng home. Yet, as the days passed he knew that he must speak. Jainu had come to occupy his waking thoughts almost as constantly as Poppy had done.

Master Peng was not as difficult to approach as Yi Wan had feared. In fact, as soon as Yi Wan broached the subject, he burst out with a laugh.

'You have been making a mountain out of this, my boy,' he said. 'Hi told me that you were interested.'

'Then may I speak to Jainu?'

'Of course.'

The Pengs had the grace and tact that Yi Wan had found in Master Su's house. They made a point of inviting him to tea one afternoon, and then leaving him alone with Jainu. He knew that this was his opportunity.

'Has your father told you that I have spoken with him?' he asked.

Jainu smiled.

'Yes,' she said softly.

'Do you care for me? Could you consider me as a possible husband?'

'I should need time to think,' she answered. 'Of course, I like you, Yi Wan. Of course, I am conscious of the honour you do me. But it is such a short time since ...'

She broke off, and Yi Wan gently laid his hand on her's.

'I understand,' he said. 'Hi Peng has told me. Perhaps we may see each other sometimes. Perhaps walk in the Park. Perhaps go out for a meal occasionally.'

'That would be agreeable,' Jainu answered.

Yi Wan knew that he must not rush his courtship of Jainu.

She had suffered, as he had once suffered, and because of his experience, he could enter into her's. He made a practice of calling at their home even earlier on Saturdays. Jainu and he would then go for a walk, or sit in the garden if the weather was warm enough. After the evening meal, she would leave him to his inevitable game of 'Go' with her father. It was necessary to keep father happy, she told him, and though Yi Wan would infinitely have preferred to spend his time with her, he saw the wisdom of her remark.

There was one fine park in Changan, just across the river, before the climb to the Emperor's palace, and when the Spring crocuses were at their best, Yi Wan took Jainu there. The chestnut trees were in full leaf, lining the walk that led to the lake and the miniature waterfall. They walked hand in hand, like any other boy and girl, and Yi Wan felt for the first time in his life that his cares were being lifted from his shoulders. He was young; he was resilient; and even though he had suffered, he felt confident that he would survive, and would find happiness.

They had brought scraps of food to feed the ducks on the lake, and joined other visitors and children on the bridge over the stream, who were doing the same thing. The sun shone in a brilliantly blue sky, and there was a general feeling abroad that all was right with the world. People were happier than they had ever been, under the wise rule of the new Emperor. Everyone knew his place in the scheme of things, and Yi Wan was coming to feel that acceptance was the key to happiness.

He wanted to embrace Jainu, and as soon as he could, he manoeuvred her away from the crowd by the lake, and led her down a path amongst flower beds, to the shaded walk by the stream. Here it was comparatively deserted, apart from other couples like themselves.

Yi Wan was aware of Jainu's frail beauty. He wondered that he could ever have thought her old or sad. She was naturally grieving when he had first met her, but she was not of a sad disposition. In fact, when they were out together, she showed an impish sense of fun.

He held her hand as they walked, and gradually slowed their pace to a halt, so that he could take her in his arms.

'Someone will see, Yi Wan,' she protested.

'Not here,' he said, linking his arms behind her.

Her bones seemed as small as a bird's, her figure like the finest and most delicate porcelain. He kissed her gently on the lips; then more firmly.

'I love you, Jainu,' he said. 'Have you thought of what I asked your father? Have you had time to consider?'

She threw her arms around his neck, pulling his face down to her's, kissing him harder.

'I will marry you, Yi Wan,' she said.

His grip on her tightened, and his kisses became more passionate as they wandered from her lips to her hair, her eyes, her throat, her ears. Through the thin-ness of their Spring garments, he could feel her firm nipples. It stirred him sexually, but he knew it would be unthinkable to show such desires before marriage.

That evening, he told Master Peng that Jainu had agreed to become his wife.

'I am glad,' the merchant said. 'When her boy died, we were worried that Jainu would never get over the shock. You have brought back happiness into her life. Her mother and I will make all arrangements, and if you wish, I can find you a cottage, because my workers come and go. It will not be a fine house like this, but it will be big enough until you have children.'

Fourteen

Yi Wan and Jainu were married three months later. There seemed no point in waiting longer. The marriage itself was a civil ceremony before a Government registrar, but Master Peng wished it to be followed by a religious observance at the Buddhist temple in Ayu-Koang Street, and Yi Wan had no objections.

Jainu and he did not go away from Changan for a honeymoon after the ceremonies, as some newly-weds might have done. Madame Peng had prepared the wedding feast at her home, and there were several dozen guests, drawn from amongst her friends and Master Peng's business associates. If Yi Wan felt out of it, because he had no family, he was not allowed to feel so for long. He was reminded that he had gained a family, and this meant a great deal to him.

In the early evening, he took his bride to the cottage her father had provided for their first home, and when they crossed the thresh-hold, Yi Wan felt that he was really making a new beginning. Until this moment, half of him had still been in Tunhuang.

Looking through their back window, Jainu said, 'We must plant a garden.'

'Do you not like the stone garden at your home?' Yi Wan asked.

'It is symbolic and peaceful, but I prefer flowers, and I should like a pond.'

'There is a stream behind the house,' Yi Wan observed. 'Perhaps it could be diverted.'

They went outside to look at the possibilities, and were quickly absorbed in their plans. Yi Wan saw that the garden would, in fact, be bigger than Master Peng's, since their cottage backed onto open land, bounded by the stream which ran down to the river.

Coming back into the house, he sank down onto the big settee.

'Do you want some supper?' Jainu asked, hovering in the kitchen doorway. 'Or something to drink?'

'No thank you,' Yi Wan answered.

'Then should we not go upstairs?'

Not until she asked, did Yi Wan realize that he had been postponing this moment, without being conscious he was doing so. He was suddenly shy in the presence of his bride, and anxious that he might not come up to her expectations in bed. It was not that he did not want to make love to her. He had dreamt of nothing else for days. But now that the time had come, he was beset with self-doubt.

Sensing his difficulty, she came over to him.

'Kiss me,' she said.

As soon as Yi Wan took her in his arms, his desire surfaced strongly, driving out all his fears as she had known it would.

'Come on,' he told her.

In the bedroom, she sat before a mirror, and taking out pins let down her hair. Yi Wan stood behind her chair, his hands caressing her shoulders. She turned to look up at him, with such an expression of love on her face that he bent to kiss her again. He put his hands on her breasts. They were small and firm, and as he fondled them, he felt the nipples harden in his palms. He realized that he already had a firm erection, and was horrified that he might ejaculate before they had even started to make love.

'Let's get undressed,' he said, pulling off his shirt and loosening the belt that held his trousers.

Jainu drew the heavy blue curtains across the window, shutting out the last of the evening light. They were now just shadows in the room. She slipped out of her kimono, and he gathered her in his arms, planting a kiss on her mouth before she could protest. Feeling her naked body against his drove him wild with desire, and as his kisses wandered feverishly from her lips to her body, all shyness dropped from them, and she began to respond actively.

When they lay on the bed, she guided his hand to her thigh. 'Here,' she said.

Guided by her knowledge, Yi Wan began to arouse her, and knowing the effect he was having on her, his own need increased unbearably.

'Don't let me come. Don't let me come,' he groaned.

When his need was at its peak, she turned onto her back and, raising her knees, opened her legs for his entry. He thrust into her savagely, and she gave a little cry of pain, but Yi Wan could no more have stopped than he could have flown.

His pounding pulsating blood told him that it would be all over in a second, and he wanted to go on, for her sake as well as for his own. Suddenly, when he felt he could bear to hold back no longer, she reached over his thigh and gently cradled his testicles in her tiny hand. The slight pressure took away the immediacy of his climax, and his thrusting continued. At last she was ready, and with a release that was almost painful in its exquisite pleasure, she let him go, and he shot and shot his sperm high inside her.

Exhausted and sweating as if he had fought three men, he rolled to her side. Her hands caressed his shoulders and chest, as she kissed him gently.

'That was wonderful,' she said.

Yi Wan had imagined the sexual act so often when he had felt the need for a woman, but nothing he had dreamt had been like the reality. He felt that this was the ultimate physical experience, and that nothing would ever be as good again, unless it were to repeat it. His body knew a satisfaction so deep that it seemed for the first time he was at peace with himself.

'It was you who made it wonderful,' he said, at last. 'I would have come too soon. Where did you learn to make love?'

'Mothers teach their daughters,' Jainu answered. 'There are techniques.'

'Like controlling premature ejaculation?' Yi Wan asked, glad that she had been taught these techniques.

'Yes. Take it more quietly, and when you think you cannot wait any longer, think of something else and stop whatever you are doing to me. That will delay your climax.'

Already Yi Wan wanted her again, and learning from her, he began to arouse her more slowly, controlling himself as she had instructed. He had a lot to learn about the art of making love, he thought, but he had the rest of his life to learn.

Wen Di had told Yi Wan that he need not come into work for the rest of the week, and Yi Wan used the time to set about making the garden that Jainu wanted. Stripped to the waist, he dug into the rich soil, hoed and planted, and made a channel to divert the stream through their back fence and down a small waterfall into a pond.

They made love every night. Each time Yi Wan felt a new satisfaction, and each night they explored new ways to give each other maximum pleasure. It was only when he was alone that Yi Wan wished he was sharing these experiences with Poppy.

At the beginning of the following week, he returned to work, and from then on, he was in his consulting room from ten to six, then home to tea, and off to the martial arts school until nine, before returning home at half past ten. At seven, he had to get up, to prepare for the next day's work.

After the first week, Jainu waited in vain for him to make love to her. Yi Wan was simply so exhausted that when he lay down, he fell asleep in seconds, and it was not until the following Sunday, which was his one day off, that he showed interest in her again.

'You are doing too much,' she told him. 'Father does not work as hard as you do and he has his own business. Wen Di gives you too many patients.'

'He sees just as many himself.'

'Perhaps you should set up practice on your own. What does Wen Di pay you? Only an assistant's salary. If you had your own practice, you could charge what you liked. Perhaps you could even employ an assistant to take some of the work off your shoulders.'

'I owe a debt to Wen Di,' Yi Wan answered. 'When I first arrived in Changan, I did not know anyone. I had only Master Su's letter, and Wen Di's address. He did not have to help me, because I was a complete stranger to him. He could have turned me away, and I would have been hard put to it, even to make a living.'

'You have repaid him many times since,' Jainu said.

She did not press the matter at that time, but in the weeks that followed, she was to return to it many times. Sometimes she felt that, although she knew that Yi Wan loved her and no-one else, he was not whole-heartedly her's. His medical work and his teaching took first place in his life.

One day, when visiting her father, she asked her brother to speak to Yi Wan about this.

'Yi Wan is a wonderful man,' he answered. 'He is both a doctor and a teacher of Wu Shu. A doctor has to be at the service of his patients.'

'And a Wu Shu master?'

'He must keep up his practice. Rival teachers can challenge him. Then the survival of his academy and perhaps his own life will depend on his skill.'

'I have married a career man,' Jainu reflected sadly.

'None the less, I will speak to him,' her brother promised.

Master Peng also took Yi Wan to task.

'You never find time for our games of Go, these days,' he grumbled.

Yi Wan felt himself pulled this way and that, and not knowing how best to respond, he did nothing, and they drifted along until the Autumn.

It was not until he arrived home one evening to find Jainu in tears that Yi Wan understood how badly his marriage was going wrong.

'What is the matter, my dearest?' he asked, full of solicitude.

Jainu quickly dried her eyes. She had not wanted Yi Wan to find her crying and she tried to make light of it.

'Nothing,' she said. 'I am just being silly.'

His medical training taught him not to accept that statement at face value.

He put his arms around Jainu.

'I am sorry if I have neglected you, my dear,' he said. 'It is not because I do not love you, but because I am so very busy.'

'You are always busy.'

'Yes,' Yi Wan soothed, 'but I mean to be more considerate.'

Even as he spoke, he wondered how this would be possible.

'What made you cry?' he pressed.

'Most married women would have a baby on the way by now,' she said.

'We have tried,' Yi Wan pointed out, 'and we shall be blessed one day.'

'Yes, we have tried,' she answered scornfully. 'Once a week, if you are not too tired, or if a patient does not call.'

Yi Wan's pride was hurt. Was she saying that he was unsatisfactory as a lover? He felt an immediate need to prove himself.

'If that's what you want,' he said harshly, 'get your clothes off.'

When she was slow to respond, he helped her roughly, and took her there and then, savagely. If it was painful, that was her fault, he thought. Later, he was full of remorse. He had acted no better than the braggarts who would challenge a Wu Shu master. He had shown the same desire to prove himself. Such desire rose from self-doubt. A master should be above such doubts. He should never need to show his prowess.

Humbly, the next morning, he told Jainu that he would speak to Wen Di about the possibility of branching out into his own practice.

Fifteen

'Why do you wish to leave?' Wen Di asked. 'You have your own consulting room; you have clinical freedom.'

'My wife complains ...'

'Ah, your wife,' Wen Di interrupted. 'Of course she is the daughter of Master Peng, and accustomed to luxury. Well, we must see.'

Later that day, Wen Di surprised Yi Wan by offering him a junior partnership, and suggesting they engage an assistant to lighten the work load. Jainu was pleased.

'He is not being over-generous with terms,' she said, 'but it is clear he doesn't want to lose you.'

'I will let Hi Peng take some of my evening classes,' Yi Wan went on. 'I can put in some of my own practice in the day.'

Jainu conceded that this was a fair arrangement, and their life settled down to an even tenor. As soon as the new assistant was engaged, Yi Wan arranged to see patients in the mornings only, transferring some to the new man. He then went to the Wu Shu academy in the afternoons, and had evenings free to spend with Jainu. He was also able to resume his weekly visits to Master Peng for their games of Go. The new arrangements worked very well, and everyone was happy.

Suzie appeared at Yi Wan's surgery on the first morning in October. He would not have recognized her. She was an old, young woman, and Yi Wan was shocked at her appearance.

'I am sorry to trouble you, Master,' she wheezed, 'but I have nowhere else to go, and you did say to come.'

'Of course,' Yi Wan answered, hastening to place a chair for her. 'How did your bruises respond? Have you been beaten again?'

She seemed not to remember this episode, but looked in front of her with a dull despair.

'You are breathless,' Yi Wan said. 'Have you been hurrying?'

'No. I have this all the time, now.'

'Lie down on the couch, please,' Yi Wan said. 'I may be able to help you. Are you still with this man for whom you worked?'

'No. He threw me out last week.'

'Where are you living?'

'I sleep where I can find warmth.'

'No fixed abode,' Yi Wan wrote in his notes.

He himself had known this situation, many years before.

He recognized that he did not owe Suzie anything, but the sympathy that he had felt when he saw her bruises returned now, and to it was added his understanding of her present plight. He must calm his pulses so that he might examine her. He sat quietly by the couch, and began to question her further.

'You say your employer threw you out. Why was this?'

'Because I have a disease.'

'You are certainly ill, but how would he know that you have a disease?'

'Some of his customers reported that they had caught it from me.'

Yi Wan had suspected some kind of heart trouble from her breathlessness and the way her hand strayed to her chest, where she appeared to have pain. Now, he realized that it must be an advanced stage of syphillis. There would be few outward symptoms, if it had proceeded thus far. The sores that betokened its onset would have cleared away. The rash and the warts that sometimes followed would have disappeared. Perhaps in her ignorance, this girl would have thought this was the end of the matter. After all, the disease was a hazard of her profession. The probability now, however, was that her heart was permanently affected. He would need to make a pulse diagnosis to be sure.

He decided to defer questioning her further until he had done this.

'Have you eaten today?' he asked.

'No, master.'

'Nor yesterday, I fear. You will need to keep up your strength. When I have taken your pulse, I will send out for food and drink, while I take your history.'

'My history?'

'I shall want to know all about you, if I am to treat you successfully.'

The pulses told Yi Wan exactly what he had suspected.

'Sit up on the chair,' he said. 'First, you must have something to eat. You will feel better then.'

He rang the bell which summoned the practice servant, and gave her instructions. She brought bread and meat and tea from the kitchen.

'Eat,' Yi Wan commanded, taking his seat at the writing desk.

'You are good to me,' Suzie said. 'Why should you care about me? I was not able to help you.'

Yi Wan did not answer her question. How could he? How could anyone explain the need to be kind? Compassion was part of his nature. He knew he should feel disgusted at her profession; he knew that she had gone on practising it and infecting the innocent, long after she must have known that the disease was in her; but he could not feel much sympathy for the men who would seek her services, though he had almost done so himself.

'How long have you been working for your employer?' he asked.

'Two years, master.'

'And did he have other girls?'

'A dozen. We are supposed to be examined every month, but my employer did not bother.'

A casual pimp and not an organized brothel keeper, Yi Wan thought. Two years ago, he would not have known that such institutions and such men flourished in China. They were things that were said to exist in foreign countries, at the far end of the Silk Road. Since he had come to Changan and to Wen Di's practice, he had learned a lot. He had treated many men.

'How did you come into this profession? Was there not some other work you could have done?'

'My father sold me to Pei Su for a great sum. I was a very attractive girl when I was young.'

Yi Wan only took in two words of this answer.

'Sold you to whom?' he demanded.

'To Pei Su. He was my employer. Do not be angry with me, master. Have I said something wrong?'

'No, Suzie, you have said nothing wrong, and I am not angry,' Yi Wan answered, letting out his breath in a long sigh. 'Your father and Pei Su are the ones who are in the wrong.'

Since he had been in Changan, Yi Wan had wondered why he had never heard of Pei Su nor encountered him. Perhaps it was not surprising that they had not actually met, for Changan was a big city, but he would have expected to have heard someone speak of Master Su's son. After all, Pei had hoped to enter the civil service at one time. He had studied at the University. As a martial artist, even though stripped of his grade, he probably practised in some obscure club. Many people must know him or know of him.

That he had sunk to living off the earnings of prostitutes saddened Yi Wan, because, although he did not have any reason to care what happened to Pei, he did care that Master Su would be distressed. Su still occupied a high place in Yi Wan's affection.

'I think you do not need me to tell you what is wrong with you,' he said gently. 'You must have recognized the symptoms, when they first appeared. Why did you go on working?'

'I had to eat.'

'And now that you are no longer wanted, and have ruined your health?'

She could not answer. There was nothing she could say, and Yi Wan could not find it in his heart to judge her.

'Do you come from this city?' he asked. 'Or from the country?'

'From the city, master.'

'Are your parents still alive?'

'I believe so.'

'Will they take you in? You must have a roof over your head and regular food. You must rest and take things easily. I can only give you a herbal treatment that will ease your pains. You should have come to me sooner.'

He saw that he was talking about impossibilities as far as she was concerned. How could she eat regular meals and take things easily?

'My father has many mouths to feed,' she said. 'I was not his only daughter.'

'And did he sell the others?'

'I do not know. They were children when I left home.'

Yi Wan knew that he ought not to become involved with patients, other than providing what treatment he could. They had to fend for themselves. He could not take the burdens of the world on his shoulders, and, seeing that Suzie would not be able to pay for the consultation he had given her, he could say that he had already done a lot for her. But Yi Wan's conscience would not let him off this easily. Her father obviously would not take her back in her present condition. If he had been willing to sell her into such degradation for money, in the first place, he was not the sort of parent whose paternal instincts could be appealed to.

Suzie was his last patient that morning, and he debated with himself what to do. He could give her money, but it was not only money she needed; it was care.

'Wait here,' he said. 'I am going to speak to my colleague.'

Wen Di's advice was exactly what Yi Wan had expected.

'Don't get involved. I do not mind your giving free

treatments occasionally. The practice has always done that. But let that be the limit.'

Yi Wan made up his mind.

'You may sit here quietly until I return,' he told Suzie. 'I am going out for a few minutes. When I come back I will make up your medicine.'

His home lay two streets from the surgery. He could be there and back in ten minutes. He was sure Jainu would share his concern.

Afterwards, he wondered if it was the fact that he was late for dinner that made his wife so cross. Little things often sparked rows. His suggestion that they might provide a temporary lodging for a patient in their spare room drove her wild with fury.

'We are not a lodging house,' she screamed. 'Are there no inns, or hospitals, if this patient is so ill? What about the relatives?'

'She has no money. She will die in the streets.'

'She? Are you mad, Yi Wan? I thought you were talking about a man. Do you really expect me to allow you to bring a woman into this house? Be she patient or not, she is not coming here. What would the neighbours say? What would my friends think?'

'She will die if she is not properly cared for.'

'So? Am I a nurse? Do I not give my husband to these patients, hours and hours every week? You think more of them than you do of me.'

'I have been taking more time off recently.'

But Yi Wan saw that his cause was hopeless, and he turned away, sick at heart that Jainu could be so callous. If she saw Suzie, perhaps she would relent, he thought, but then he knew better.

'I will be home in about twenty minutes,' he told her.

The only other possibility he could think of was his old lodging house. Perhaps, if he offered to pay, his landlady would take Suzie in, until something else could be arranged. He had a feeling it would not be for long, anyway. Surely, for such a short time, Jainu could have co-operated!

The walk to his former lodgings took longer than Yi Wan had expected, and it was half an hour before he was back in his consulting room. He found Suzie anxious, and embarrassed at being there. She was afraid the servants were looking down on her, or that one of the other doctors would come in and tell her to go. She had not been used to kindness.

It was this that touched Yi Wan most about her case.

'I have arranged a room for you to stay,' he told her. 'It is only an attic, but there is a bed and facilities for washing and so on. The landlady will give you meals. I want you to rest as much as you can. I will give you a medicine to take when the pain is severe, but rest is the only cure. I need not warn you against attempting to go with men. You would be thrown out of your lodging at once, and I could not be responsible for you again. Come with me.'

'But who will pay? I have no money, and if I do not earn!'

Yi Wan saw that she still hoped to make her living by the practice of her profession, though she would no longer be under the protection of her employer and though her looks had long faded. This was what these girls usually came to, in the end, and that end was usually swift. The organisers of prostitution did not welcome free-lance rivals.

'You must not worry about money. I will pay for your lodging for the next few weeks at least, and then we shall see what happens. But you must give me your solemn promise that you will not seek clients.'

Yi Wan had not told her all that he knew. Those few weeks would see the end of her troubles. A roof and care were the least he could provide, for the little time she had left.

His old landlady had let the room that Yi Wan had occupied, and the attic to which she took Suzie was a much inferior room, but to her it was a palace, and Yi Wan knew that she would be well fed.

'I cannot give you anything in return,' Suzie told him. 'Even my body. You could have had that, when I was young and pretty, but you did not want me then. Remember?'

'Put the past behind you,' Yi Wan said, 'and do not worry. You will be safe here, and I will come and see you in a week.'

But Yi Wan did not go then.

Three days earlier, a woman waited outside his treatment room, and caught up with him as he left.

'Excuse me, doctor.'

'Yes. What is it?'

'Are you the doctor who treated Suzie?'

'Yes.'

'I called to see her this morning. She had got word to me as to where she was living. She is much worse.'

'You worked with her?' Yi Wan asked.

'Yes.'

'Then let her condition be a lesson to you. It is the inevitable end of what you do.'

'Pei Su would find us if we left him. Only one girl ever ran away. She was taken from the river with knife wounds. Many wounds. She had died slowly.'

'I will see Suzie,' Yi Wan said.

He had a feeling of utter helplessness as far as this problem was concerned. As long as there were men who would pay for sex, there were women who would supply it. If not Suzie, or this girl, then some other.

Leaving the girl, he hurried to the lodging house, but he was too late. Suzie had died of an aneurysm of the aorta, just as Yi Wan had foreseen she would.

Sixteen

'Where have you been?' Jainu demanded, when Yi Wan arrived home late for lunch.

'To see a patient.'

Yi Wan was sick at heart at what had happened to Suzie, and at Jainu's refusal to take her in.

'Why could he not come to the treatment room?'

'It was not a man. It was the young girl of whom I spoke to you. She was too ill to leave her bed.'

'So you visit young girls in their home! What do you think I feel about that? First, you are too tired to make love to me properly, and we do not have children like other families. Then you treat patients all day and want to practice fighting all evening. Then you ask me to nurse your patients here, and finally you tell me you visit young girls at home.'

'Please Jainu, only one girl, and she was no longer young.'

'What did she mean to you?'

'She was a patient, nothing more. Please do not say any more, Jainu. She died this morning.'

'So you can stay with me this afternoon, and go to your Academy this evening?'

Yi Wan knew what she was asking, but he did not want to make love to her that afternoon. He wondered if he ever would again. These days he found himself thinking more and more about Poppy.

It was on the way home from the Wu Shu academy that he was attacked. He was entering the shadow cast by the warehouse buildings, when his senses alerted him to danger.

121

Hi Peng had left him only ten minutes before. His senses were not sight or hearing, but a kind of sixth sense that Master Su had told him he would develop.

A black-garbed figure leaped from the wall, his sword cleaving the air, in a two-handed downcut. The blade was of tempered steel and sharp as a razor. Yi Wan had seen such swords used to sever a bullock's head at one swipe. He did not see the sword; he did not see the man. His body made the right-hand turn without any conscious direction on his part, and the blade whistled past him. Yi Wan's left forearm went across the assailant's windpipe, and he clasped the man's wrist in his right hand and pulled the arm back against his right thigh.

He would simply have applied an armlock and stranglehold to discourage further attack, if he had not caught the sense of another attacker. It then became imperative to put the first one out of the way. Yi Wan raised his left forearm slightly in a swift movement, and he heard the man's neck snap. As he dropped the body, the other man stabbed at his left side, inwards and upwards, with a short dagger. The blade was meant to pierce Yi Wan's heart, but again he side-stepped, and with a chop to the throat and a kick to the knee, he laid the man out. His knee was dislocated; he would not get up again. And he was choking with the blow on his windpipe.

'Ah, I see that you remember what my father taught you.'

At this moment, a tall figure stepped from the shadows, where he had waited to see the despatch of his victim. It was Pei Su.

Yi Wan would not have recognized him. Pei Su had now grown fatter and he was completely bald. He was none-the-less dangerous. Yi Wan remembered that he had been a graduate of Master Su's, before stripped of his title, and Master Su did not give out certificates easily, even to his own son.

All Yi Wan's revulsion at what had happened to Suzie rose in his mind. To this was added his disgust at Pei's profession, and at the way he had let his father down. He thought he had put Poppy's case behind him, but he knew now that what had happened to her at Pei's hands still had power to hurt. Hatred welled up in his heart, like blood from a wound. He wanted to kill Pei at that moment, yet he knew that if he was to have any chance of survival himself, he must control this emotion. Anger clouded judgement, and made breathing shallow. Shallow breathing weakened the force of attack. Tension prepared a man to meet the attack he was expecting; it did not allow enough fluidity of movement to cope with the unexpected.

Yi Wan called to mind his Shaolin breathing exercises, and putting away all thought of anger or of what Pei had done to those whom he loved, Yi Wan stilled his mind and his heart.

'I heard that you were considered a good pupil of my father,' Pei went on. 'Perhaps we shall see how good.'

'What do you want with me?' Yi Wan answered, loath to fight Su's son, since Su was the first man who had shown kindness to him.

'You told one of my girls that Suzie's fate would befall her and all the others, if they continued to follow their calling. I do not like people interfering with my girls, and giving them ideas like that. Not that they will take any notice of what you have said. I know how to deal with girls who disobey me, or who do not bring in their nightly quota of earnings. But you are one of those busybodies who cannot mind their own business, and am I to be thwarted or put to inconvenience by a gardener's boy on whom my father took pity?'

His rush would have taken Yi Wan by surprise, if he had not been calm. Pei Su scorned weapons, and came in with both fists and knees in a four-pronged attack. Yi Wan blocked three of the attacks, but the fist that smashed into his ribcage was like an iron hammer and it hurt. If he had not already been turning away from the blow, several ribs would have been smashed. Fat and old, Pei Su might be, but he was deadly. He swirled, like a dancer, and came back with high kicks to the face, which Yi Wan deflected upwards. Then the short kick with the top of the foot to the testicles. This alone could finish off the opponent, if it was delivered correctly. An elbow strike to the kidneys followed. Yi Wan automatically avoided all these attacks, but he knew that he was being forced into fighting a defensive battle. Fights were never won by defensive tactics alone. Shaolin had taught him that. He had to go in, to win, even if he sacrificed an arm or an eye to do so.

His first counter that got through was a back fist strike to the heart. Pei Su gasped and turned away, but immediately spun completely round and came back with a chop to the temple. Ducking, Yi Wan planted a reverse punch in Pei's solar plexus. This was the nerve centre of the body, and it should have stopped him, but although Pei grunted with pain, he came on. His attacks did not lose their speed or power. Yi Wan saw that he was unstoppable, except by the Shaolin spirit.

Breathing deeply, he came under Pei's murderous attacks, in and up, with a counter delivered with the second knuckles of the right hand. Formed by bending the fingers towards the palm, these knuckles presented a spade-shaped attacking edge that caught Pei on the throat, smashing through his windpipe. The blow lifted Pei from the ground, and as he fell backwards blood poured from his mouth. He was dead when he fell, and the expression of astonishment had still not left his face.

Sweating and trembling with the reaction, Yi Wan examined the bodies of his other assailants. They were dead.

Then he turned back to the main road. It was his duty to go to the office of the civil guard and to report the matter.

Just before coming into the main street, Yi Wan spotted the girl who had called him to Suzie. At first he thought she was soliciting, but she had been looking out for him.

'Pei Su is seeking you,' she said urgently. 'He has two thugs with him.'

'I know,' Yi Wan answered. 'Thank you for the warning, but I am on my way to report that the attack was unsuccessful.'

'And is Pei dead?'

'Yes.'

'I am glad.'

When he reached home, after reporting the incident, his

ribs were hurting, and he told Jainu what had happened.

'That's what comes of interfering in the lives of people who do not concern you,' she retorted, but when she saw his bruises, she immediately became more sympathetic.

'Oh, my darling, can I do anything?'

Yi Wan examined his own injuries, probing gently. He had been lucky. No bones were broken.

'Fetch me the jar of salve from the bedroom,' he said.

Two days later, Yi Wan was summoned to the office of the civil guard.

'I have to give you this notice, requiring you to appear in the Magistrates Court, on the seventeenth of this month,' the clerk on duty told him.

'But why?' Yi Wan demanded.

'You are to be charged with killing the three citizens named thereon.'

'But it was they who attacked me, and I reported the incident.'

'None the less, killing is a serious matter.'

When Yi Wan told his wife and Hi Peng, they both had the same advice.

'Speak with our father.'

'You do not understand the ways of our city,' Master Peng said sadly. 'The man you killed – Pei Su – was probably a member of the Tangs. They are a secret society that bedevils our city. They can put pressure on the government, on the civil guard, on the magistrates.'

'Then what must I do?'

'Leave it to me,' Master Peng answered.

At first, Yi Wan had felt no worry as to what might happen to him, though he had been horrified that it was Master Su's own son whom he had killed, but as the seventeenth of the month drew near, he felt drained of strength. Enemies who fought with fist or foot or weapon, he could deal with. Enemies who fought with secret bribes were beyond his comprehension, and a thousand times more dangerous.

Seventeen

It seemed odd to Yi Wan that two days before his trial, Jainu suddenly became more cheerful about his prospects.

'Don't worry any more,' she said, when he came home to lunch. 'Everything is going to be all right.'

Hi Peng was equally confident, when they met in the training hall, and the very next morning, the clerk from the civil guard's office came to the consulting rooms.

'Honoured master,' he began, when Yi Wan called him in. 'I have been sent to apologise. There has been a mistake. You are not to be charged. We know you acted in self defence, and we have to thank you for reporting the incident and for freeing our city of these dangerous thugs.'

Yi Wan did not know which emotion was uppermost, relief or astonishment. He saw two more patients as soon as he was calm enough, and was sterilising his needles when Wen Di came in.

'The case against me has been dropped,' he said.

'Ah yes.'

There was a look of inner knowledge on Wen Di's face that told Yi Wan he had never feared any other outcome. Recently Jainu and Hi Peng had shown the same confidence.

'You are the son-in-law of Master Peng, aren't you,' Wen Di explained.

Wen Di's words took away nearly all Yi Wan's happiness. It was not justice that had saved him, but the influence of someone even more powerful than Pei Su's friends.

For days this thought troubled him, until it was driven from his mind by an event of much greater magnitude.

126

In the middle of morning surgery, Wen Di called him into his own consulting room. This was something that had never occurred before, during their association. A young man lay on the couch. He was unnaturally pale, and even as they approached him, he raised himself up, and said, 'Doctor, I must go to the toilet.'

'Of course,' Wen Di replied, 'to the left, as you leave the room.'

When he had gone, Wen Di showed the notes he had made.

'There is no doubt, is there?' he asked.

'Dry tongue, dark yellow urine samples, very little urine passed but frequent defecation, said to be like muddy water, according to the patient.'

'How about skin elasticity?' Yi Wan asked.

'None. I have tried pinching the skin over the abdomen.'

'What district is he from?'

'Choku. It is down by the river. A warren of poor houses.'

Yi Wan understood Wen Di's need to be certain, and his hope that he might have been mistaken, but there was no doubt.

'I agree,' Yi Wan said. 'It is cholera.'

'It will run like wildfire through that community. The man may have caught it from polluted water, or from fruit or vegetables. We must report it to the city authorities, of course. In the meantime, you are a medical herbalist. Is there anything you would give?'

Yi Wan shook his head. In cases of cholera, the needles were ineffective, nor did he know of any herbs that would save the patient from dehydration and certain death. In telling Wen Di that the only hope was to maintain the patient's fluid intake at a high level, Yi Wan knew he was not saying something that the other man did not know.

'Adding powdered rice to the water may help,' he said. 'At least it acts as a placebo, and the patient is given hope.'

'But if he contracted the disease from drinking polluted water, then more water from the same source will only make things worse.'

Yi Wan could only agree, and when the patient returned, he left Wen Di to tell the young man, and went back to his own consulting room.

Hurrying home at the end of the morning, he told Jainu that she must boil every drop of water they used, even for cooking or washing.

'Don't touch raw fruit unless you first wash it in boiling water and then peel it,' he said. 'And if you feel the slightest tendency to diarrhoea, tell me at once.'

'What is it?' she asked, alarmed at his urgency.

'Cholera,' he said. 'We must tell your father at once, but do not spread the news further or there will be panic in the streets.'

Whilst Jainu finished preparing lunch, Yi Wan ran to Master Peng's house and told him. Perhaps, with the influence that had secured his own pardon, Master Peng could persuade the authorities to act in this situation as well. Whether by reason of that influence or of Wen Di's warning, the government took the outbreak seriously, and the next morning Wen Di told Yi Wan that the town crier had been warning people in the Choku district to boil their drinking water.

'But already I have eight more cases,' he added.

The next day reports came in of a hundred victims, and by the afternoon, the figure had risen to a thousand. The Emperor published a decree, declaring the Choku district a disaster area, and requiring all who possessed medical qualifications to go there. Wen Di sent messages to all their patients, and the practice closed down.

'There is nothing we can do,' Yi Wan said, when told of the Imperial decree. 'There is simply no cure. Unless you can replace the fluid the patient is losing every hour, death from dehydration is inevitable. It takes only eight or nine hours.'

'We can advise and comfort,' Wen Di answered, and Yi Wan saw that this was also the role of a physician.

What was really needed was an Imperial decree ordering the clean-up of the river. That was where all these people obtained their water supply, and it was the dumping ground for sewage, for dead cats and dogs, and for any other rubbish that people wanted to get rid of in a hurry.

Yi Wan had never been to the Choku district. In fact he had not ventured far outside the central sector of the town where his father-in-law lived and where he had his practice and his school. He was shocked by what he found.

The streets in Choku were all narrow lanes, dirty and foul-smelling. Sewage disposal was by means of open drains that led to the river. Windows that had been broken in the houses were never repaired, and with winter coming on and no heating, the houses were cold and damp. When he told a woman to boil her drinking water, she answered 'What with?' having neither fuel for a fire, nor money to buy any. When he told a patient to rest, the look of despair and the crowded rooms were sufficient answer. He began to understand how girls like Suzie drifted into their profession, or were sold by their parents, and the alternatives that made them stay in such a trade.

Even in establishments such as Pei Su had run, a girl would have a room in which to entertain clients; she would have clothes to make her attractive; she would have food. She might even be given presents on top of the fees she would have to turn over to her employer. Her life might be horrible, but it was only slightly more horrible than starving in filth, without privacy or comfort.

Wen Di, Yi Wan and their assistant worked the same streets in the Choku district. They would go down in the morning, choose houses next door to each other, and so work down the street together. There was nothing they could do for any of the patients, except to offer advice and comfort. The advice would not be taken, simply because it could not be, and Yi Wan could only hope that the words of comfort would be more effective, in soothing the patient's fears.

He soon became hardened to death. Each day, some of the people he had seen the day before would be missing. Each day, the municipal carts carried off more bodies to the common grave. What would be the end of it all, he could not guess. He only knew that there had to be an end. Nothing lasted for ever.

During these days, he abandoned even his evening practices with Hi Peng, feeling that however little he could do in practical terms for people, he must be where he was needed most. Even Jainu understood this. She was very quiet when he came home, sensing that he needed rest. She had his meals always waiting. She did not complain of anything, even when he was late, or his clothes were infected with lice from contact with the poor people he visited. She simply put out new garments and washed his old.

The only respite Yi Wan allowed himself was the Saturday evening visit to Master Peng. He felt that he owed the older man so much, that although the debt was never spoken of and hence could not be acknowledged, it was his duty to visit and to cheer. Master Peng always received Yi Wan hospitably. The Saturday evening games were his way of relaxing.

'The outbreak has been confined to one district,' he told Yi Wan on one of these occasions.

Yi Wan accepted the information without question. He was too close to the work to see the overall picture, and such information as did reach him was only rumour and hearsay. He knew that his father-in-law must have better sources.

'But what are the authorities doing to stop the epidemic?' he asked.

'What can be done? There is only education. That is where you and your fellow practitioners come in. You are telling people what they should have known long ago. Perhaps they did know and took no notice.'

'Perhaps they could not take any notice,' Yi Wan replied, knowing that it was all very well for a rich man like Master Peng to talk of hygiene in the home, and quite another thing for a man without food to feed his family to worry himself about such matters.

'The authorities are burying the dead,' Master Peng went on. 'They are arranging to feed the young children in the schools, so that they will have at least one good meal a day. Charities are doing their bit, providing pots to boil water, fuel and warm garments.'

All of which was prompted by a fear that unless something was done, the cholera would spread to other districts, and might engulf the rich, Yi Wan thought bitterly. But, whatever the reason, the outbreak was gradually brought under control. The daily figure of deaths began to fall, and Wen Di said they would soon be able to open up their practice again.

Shortly after this, Jainu told Yi Wan her good news.

'I'm going to have a baby. A son, for you, I hope.'

The look of utter happiness on her face communicated itself to Yi Wan, and he knew joy that had been missing from his life for quite a long time.

Tenderly, he took her in his arms and kissed her. She suddenly seemed so fragile and so precious.

'When will it be?' he asked.

'You are a doctor, and you ask me?' she joked. 'The usual time. Late next Summer.'

Eighteen

A few days after hearing Jainu's good news, Wen Di opened up his treatment rooms again, and Yi Wan returned to his practice. The worst of the epidemic was over. He had heard that five thousand people had perished, many of them children, but official figures were hard to come by, and this might only be a rumour. He wished that it were a disease that would have responded to his acupuncture needles, or that he had known a herb that would help, but nothing that he remembered from Master Su's teaching had been of any use. Cholera was accepted by the profession as a plague against which there was no defence. The lucky few who could pull through the crisis and replace their lost body fluids quickly survived; the others died.

Life quickly resumed its normal routine of consultations in the morning, afternoons spent with Jainu, and evenings at the Wu Shu academy, and Yi Wan felt that it was good. He was at peace with the whole world. Better still he was at peace with himself. He had resumed his happy relationship with his wife; he had been able to fulfil her dearest wish and to give her a child; he was happy to be of service to his patients, and to train young men in the fighting arts; he enjoyed his own practices with Hi Peng.

Tragedy came like a tiny cloud that suddenly expands until it fills the whole sky.

Yi Wan came back from the cosulting rooms one lunchtime to find no meal awaiting him, nor any sign of Jainu.

'Jainu,' he called. 'Jainu, I'm back.'

A faint sound from the upper room came down to him, and he ran up the stairs, two at a time.

'Jainu, what is the matter?'

She lay on the bed, white-faced and sweating. The slop bucket beside the bed was full of stinking faeces. One glance at it told Yi Wan the terrible truth. She was already passing muddy water.

'When did this start?' he asked quietly.

'An hour after you had gone.'

'Why didn't you send for me?'

'I called and called, but no-one heard, and I have been running to the toilet every few minutes. When I felt too weak to go there any more, I brought the bucket into the bedroom. I cannot control myself.'

'Don't worry, darling,' Yi Wan said. 'I will get you something.'

He knew that she must drink. It was her only hope. She would lose something like fifteen litres of fluid a day. She must already have lost four. Unless she started replacing it, she would quickly reach the danger level, and there was a point of no return. But how had she contracted the disease? Was the water unsafe, even here?

He boiled a kettle, and took her a cup of weak tea.

'Drink this.'

'I can't,' she said. 'I can't keep anything down. It all goes through. The mess ...'

'Never mind the mess. I can clear that up,' Yi Wan replied. 'Come now. Sit up and take a sip. You must, darling. You can pull through, if you will co-operate.'

'It's no use. How many of your other patients pulled through?'

'Please, darling, don't give up. Don't go away from me. I will stay with you. I will nurse you. You can get better, if you will only fight. We'll fight together.'

Sitting on the bed, he lifted her light body, and holding her up with one hand, he put the cup to her lips with the other.

Obediently she swallowed. One sip, then another, then another.

Yi Wan waited until the cup was empty before he asked 'Did you drink unboiled water?'

'No. I ate an apple, I bought some in the market. I did not peel it, because it looked so tempting and fresh.'

At least the infection had not come from his own contacts with the disease, Yi Wan thought. He was grateful for the assurance of this, because although he believed cholera was not passed on by human contact, he had never been certain, and he did not think any doctor really knew.

'You must drink, darling,' he said. 'More and more and more. I'll get rid of this bucket, and bring back a clean one. Then I'll prepare any drink you want.'

'Just plain water,' Jainu answered. 'This tea tastes so bitter.'

'That is the result of the illness,' Yi Wan told her. 'I'll be back in a few minutes.'

He emptied and scoured the bucket, washed his hands in a solution of juniper berries to disinfect them, and made a jar of boiled water, in which he placed a handful of ground rice. This gave the water a milky consistency, and was said to help the patient to retain the fluid in the stomach. With it, he carried a chair into the bedroom.

He had been hungry when he returned to the house, but now his appetite had gone, and he had no thought of anything but the need to see that Jainu drank and drank. She seemed very weak, and Yi Wan reproached himself that he had ever left her, that morning. He should have spotted some symptom, or guessed that something was amiss. He was a doctor. He was trained to look out for these things. Did he observe his patients more closely than he observed his own wife?

Jainu was too weak to argue with him, when he presented the cup to her lips. She sipped, and rested, and sipped again, until she indicated that she must get out of bed and use the pail. He was dismayed at how little urine she managed to pass, and at its dark yellow colour. Her condition was farther advanced than he had thought.

He looked out of the window, hoping to see some passer-by, whom he could send for help, but in mid-afternoon the street was empty.

'Can you hold the cup, dear?' he asked.

Jainu tried, and with the grip of both hands was able to raise it to her mouth.

'Continue sipping this,' Yi Wan said. 'I am going to see if our neighbour is at home. Perhaps she will run for help. I will be back very quickly.'

The house next door was empty, and in the one next to that there was only a small child who said his mother was out and who did not seem to understand anything else. It was not until he came to the third house that Yi Wan found anyone capable of appreciating his problem.

'A silver piece if you will run at once to Master Peng's factory, and ask him to come. His daughter is desperately ill.'

Money always produced a willingness to help, Yi Wan had found. He did not want to trust to simple good-neighbour-liness in this crisis. Often that feeling was not strong enough.

The woman whom he approached took the coin, and said she would send her son at once, but not until he had seen the lad depart, did Yi Wan return to his wife.

Jainu had sunk back apathetically onto the bed, and the empty cup rolled on the floor beside her, but whether she had drunk the contents or simply dropped the whole thing, Yi Wan could not make up his mind. He filled another cup, and raising her up, persuaded her to drink.

How long he worked alone with her, he did not know. It seemed hours before anyone came. Then suddenly, Master Peng was with him.

Yi Wan took the old man out of Jainu's hearing.

'She is far gone,' he said. 'The only hope is drink, rest, warmth and constant care.'

'I will fetch her mother and brother at once,' Master Peng replied, 'and anything else you want. Is there any doctor who specialises in this condition?'

'None,' Yi Wan answered. 'I am doing all that any other

physician could do, but call another to help if you wish.'

Master Peng went away, and Yi Wan pleaded with Jainu to drink again. He felt that she was already losing hope, because each time she drank a cup, she would have to sit on the pail, and the fluid would pass straight through her. Even with the powdered rice in it, her body was not retaining any of the water.

Yi Wan did not know what to do next. There was no other cure. If this did not work … but he could not allow himself to think of that. He ran downstairs and put another kettle to boil.

When Master Peng came back, he brought his wife and Hi Peng with him, and they were able to divide up the duties. The old man attended to the fire, boiling cauldron after cauldron of water, and setting it to cool so that it would be to Jainu's taste. Hi Peng dealt with emptying the pail. Madame Peng cleaned up the room, straightened the bed, and put a clean blanket over Jainu, who seemed more comfortable now that her family had arrived. Yi Wan saw that she drank continuously.

Evening came, and Madame Peng went downstairs to prepare a light meal for them all. Jainu could not eat, and Yi Wan felt no hunger either, but they persuaded him to take a little food.

'You above all of us must keep up your strength,' Master Peng told him. 'You are the only man who knows what to do.'

'No-one really knows,' Yi Wan answered.

They divided the night into shifts, and although Yi Wan said that he must stay with Jainu all the time, they persuaded him to take his period of rest downstairs.

'We will call you if there is any change, and any one of us can prepare drinks and see that she takes them.'

When he sank into the chair by the fire, Yi Wan was asleep in minutes. The struggle and the lack of normal nutriment had exhausted him.

Master Peng and Hi Peng had to shake him several times before he awoke.

'Where am I? What time is it?'

'Three in the morning, Yi Wan. Come. Jainu is asking for you.'

The situation suddenly came back to Yi Wan, dispelling the fog of sleep that was clouding his mind. He must get to Jainu at once. He started up the stairs.

Madame Peng stood up as he entered the room, and Yi Wan took her place at the bedside.

'Is that you, Yi Wan?' Jainu whispered. 'I cannot see you in this light.'

'I am here, Jainu,' he said, taking her hand.

'I won't be able to give you a son, now, Yi Wan. I wanted to.'

Her words were spoken so softly that Yi Wan could scarcely catch them.

'That does not matter, Jainu,' he said. 'Not now. All that I want is for you to get better, and when you are better, you will be able to give us both a son or a daughter.'

She shook her head.

The movement was as slight as the motion of a flower in the summer breeze.

'I cannot stay,' she said. 'I am so thirsty.'

'Please, drink this, my darling. I love you.'

Her lips curled upwards in a beautiful smile, and in that moment she had gone.

Yi Wan was inconsolable. He blamed himself for not noticing, before he left for work, that Jainu was ill. He blamed himself for every neglect during their months of marriage, for the times when his medical practice or the martial arts had come between them. He blamed himself for the way he had reproached her in his mind when she would not take in Suzie. He blamed himself that he had never fully been her's, that even when they made love, he had thought of Poppy. Now it was all too late.

Nineteen

'Master, have you heard of The Way of The Eagle school?'

It was a senior pupil who put the question to Yi Wan, as they were walking away from the Wu Shu academy one afternoon.

'It is one of the southern schools, isn't it?' Yi Wan answered.

'Yes, master.'

'Based on the movement of the eagle? Flapping wings to disconcert the opponent and to make entry for attack difficult, then swift jabs with the finger tips, like the beak of an eagle?'

Yi Wan had been told of this school, whilst he was studying at Shaolin. It was one of many that existed in both north and south China, each one based on the ideas of the master in charge.

'Why do you ask?' Yi Wan prompted, when the student received his answer in silence.

'They say that the master is going to demonstrate the main technique in public, by plucking the eye from a tiger. It is a feat that the first teacher of the style accomplished, in order to save himself, when attacked by the animal in the forest. People will not believe that it can be done, or that it ever was done. The present master has arranged the demonstration, not only for his own reputation, but to vindicate the claims of the founder.'

'Where is the attempt to be made?' Yi Wan demanded.

'In the city of Tai-Po.'

'How far away is that?'

'Two hundred miles, master.'

138

'And when is the demonstration to take place?'

'It has been advertised for next week. People will come from many miles around, to see if it can be done. If the master succeeds, his reputation will be greatly enhanced and his school will become one of the most famous in all China.'

'What is the master's name?' Yi Wan asked.

'Cho Ta Hung.'

The name was not familiar to Yi Wan. He guessed that the man was one of the rising generations of teachers, out to build his reputation quickly, with a spectacular display of his prowess. He was equally certain that the demonstration would be arranged so that the tiger had no chance.

It was always so, in these man versus animal fights. How could a man and an animal be equally matched? The animal would not know that it was expected to fight, and if well-fed just before the event and somnolent, it could be overcome by a swift attack, before it even realized that danger existed. The more unscrupulous masters even resorted to drugs to dull an animal's reactions, before they faced it.

This was the first time Yi Wan had ever heard of a tiger being chosen for such a demonstration. Usually, these charlatans picked on one of the small monkeys, or a young bear, or even a reptile whose fangs had been drawn. Yi Wan did not even believe the founder's claim to have saved himself in the jungle by this daring exploit. An animal's eyes were deep set and protected in their sockets. Even an eagle would find it difficult to pluck the eye of a tiger, though it might do this with a lamb or a goat. Similar rumours about the prowess of ancient teachers abounded in China. Sometimes they were started by the teacher himself; more usually they were spread by his students. The story always grew in proportion to the number of times it was repeated.

But Yi Wan's initial reaction was not to question the validity of the master's claim; it was horror. Even if the man had been skilful enough to do this thing, it seemed to Yi Wan so abominably cruel, that he felt he would never respect such a master. He had been taught to respect all life at Shaolin. If in order to save yourself from death, you had to kill an animal, it must be done swiftly and with mercy. To blind a noble creature and then allow it to escape into the jungle was absolutely repugnant to Yi Wan's nature, and went against all that he had ever been taught.

He could picture Master Su's reaction, if he heard of the event. He remembered, too, Xi Hang's story of the Buddha, and of the compassion he had shown to a starving tigress. This was the way to treat animals, as brothers and sisters, fellow creatures who were part of the all-embracing Tao, that gave life and was life and was beyond life.

'Have you heard of Cho Ta Hung?' he asked Hi Peng when they were at supper that evening.

'He is one of the southern masters. He has a high reputation.'

'Already?'

Yi Wan was surprised. He had thought they were talking about a little-known teacher. The more famous did not need to boost their reputation with deeds like this.

'Have you heard about his plan to pluck the eye from a tiger?' he asked.

'There is talk of such an attempt amongst the students. It would not surprise me if it were true. Cho Ta Hung is very swift and very skilful, and he knows this. He is said to have courage, but he is vain. If it had ever been suggested to him that he could not emulate the feat of the founder of his system, he would be compelled to try. That is his nature.'

'Then do you think this is more than just student talk?'

Hi Peng nodded his head.

'Do you know the road to Tai-Po?' Yi Wan asked.

'I can find out. It is on one of the trade routes. Father has a map in his office. What are you thinking, Yi Wan?'

'I am going to stop the demonstration.'

'How will you do that?'

'By challenging Cho Ta Hung myself. A master cannot refuse a challenge by another accredited master.'

'True, but think carefully, Yi Wan. You may not have

heard of Cho Ta Hung before today, but he is not some upstart. He is a man who has a high reputation amongst martial artists. His school has many adherents. I have actually met some of his pupils. They came to a school where I was studying before I joined up with you. All Cho Ta Hung's pupils have the same characteristic qualities. They baffle their opponents by whirling their arms at great speed, like the flapping wings of some great bird. Sometimes their movements are so fast that you seem to see not two but six or eight arms, and it is impossible to pick out the real ones from the images. Then, suddenly, a claw will shoot out at your face or body.'

'Then how old is Cho Ta Hung? If you have seen his students, four years ago or more, he must be middle-aged at least.'

'He would be in his late forties or early fifties. He is in the prime of his life. There are the usual stories about him. Some say that he was a child genius, who showed such great promise that his master accepted him into the school at the age of ten, a thing never before heard of in Wu Shu academies.'

Yi Wan respected Hi Peng's assessment of the teacher. Hi Peng was not given to exaggeration. Cho Ta Hung would be the most dangerous opponent Yi Wan had ever met. Yet he knew that he had no choice but to challenge the man. If he did not try to stop this contest, he would never be able to live with his conscience. His interference with events now was prompted by the same spirit that had made him fight to save the kitten, on the day that Master Su had found him. He could not tolerate unnecessary suffering, least of all when its only purpose was to satisfy the ego of a teacher. He saw the demonstration as being against the principles of the really great masters, like Li Su and against the Shaolin tradition.

'Hi Peng, will you come with me?' he asked.

'Yes master, but let us take three or four of our senior students.'

'Will that be necessary?'

'The road is dangerous. It passes through the mountains. You want to arrive in Tai-Po, don't you? Bandits are less likely to stop a group than two isolated travellers.'

'How long will the journey take?'

'By horse? Five or six days. The road is very lonely, but there are inns and stabling along the route, because trade caravans do go that way to the southern ports.'

'Then choose our companions tonight, and let us set out at dawn.'

Hi Peng felt it would be disrespectful to argue with Yi Wan, and he did what he had been asked to do, but he was unhappy about the matter. He had noticed that since Jainu's death, Yi Wan had become wild in his practice. He was careless of injury to himself, although he still took care not to hurt any of his students. It seemed to Hi Peng that Yi Wan's life had become less important to him. He did not appear to feel pain, and pushed himself to unnecessary extremes when using the punching boards. The only time that Yi Wan seemed to recover his former calm was when he set out for his morning consultations at Wen Di's treatment centre.

Hi Peng could see that Yi Wan still blamed himself for Jainu's death. It was unnecessary. Nothing could have saved her. There was simply no cure for cholera. But no amount of reassurance could convince Yi Wan of that. He felt he had not done all he should.

When Hi Peng visited the homes of the pupils he thought would be most useful on the journey, all of them agreed to come. He put a senior man in charge of classes while they were away; he cancelled his lessons with private pupils; he sent to Wen Di and told him of Yi Wan's impending absence; he arranged the hire of horses from the livery stables. He could not trust Yi Wan to think of all these things for himself, because the latter was often lost to the world, these days, as he retreated within himself.

Such was Master Peng's standing in the town, that all his son's arrangements went forward smoothly, and at dawn horses and travelling companions were at the door. Yi Wan himself loaded his weapons and his practice suit onto the pack animal. A master who was challenged had the right to choose weapons if he wished, and Yi Wan wanted his own sword and staff to be available. He did not think Cho Ta Hung would choose to fight with either, however. Most Wu Shu masters were too proud of their ability in unarmed fighting to resort to weaponry. They considered that was only for the military or for brigands. There was a tradition that a really skilled master could even overcome an armed opponent without resorting to weapons himself.

The little party rode through the streets of Changan in the cool before sunrise. Yi Wan had not realized it was such a large city. He thought it had developed since he was brought to the outskirts as a child captive. He had never been a man to wander about the town, however. Work and his home life had filled all his hours.

Now that he had embarked on this venture, he felt calm. He knew it was no use dwelling on the cruelty which he wanted to prevent. That would only make him angry, and anger could be his downfall. Nor was it profitable to think of the reputation of Cho Ta Hung. If you thought an opponent was your superior, you had lost the fight before it was begun. You had to believe in success, and go out whole-heartedly to achieve it. These were the things Shaolin had taught him. These were the things he must remember now. His only anxiety was that they might not reach Tai-Po in time.

Once they had left the city, the road turned into the foothills of a lofty range of mountains. The party followed a stony path that led through a gorge, and then climbed to a pass with a breath-taking view of mountains ahead, snow-capped even at this time of the year. Twice they passed through small villages of adobe huts thatched with leaves, where ragged and bare-footed children ran out to stare at them. Then, they were in wild country, with no human habitation in sight.

For the next four days they were in hill country. It was heavily pitted with gorges, and sometimes they had to make a detour of fifteen miles to avoid an abyss. By day, the sun blazed down with a merciless glare; by night the temperature was sub-zero. But Hi Peng knew the route, and had planned their stopping places with care, so that they were never exposed to the night elements, and so that Yi Wan would arrive fresh.

When they neared Tai-Po, farms and villages were more in evidence, and Yi Wan saw that the town was an important provincial centre. Their last stop was at an inn some twenty miles from the city, and the inn-keeper could talk of nothing else but the coming exhibition.

'It has emptied my house of customers,' he said. 'Everyone is going into Tai-Po, and I wish I could go myself.'

'Then is the demonstration this evening?' Yi Wan asked anxiously.

'No, tomorrow. The Provincial Governor will be present. It is something you will not see again in your lifetime. Is that why you are going to Tai-Po, Master?'

'Yes,' Yi Wan answered simply.

He was not going to tell the man the real purpose of his journey.

'Then you must leave at dawn, or you will not get a seat. The spectacle is scheduled for the early afternoon. The Governor has declared the day a public holiday.'

Yi Wan agreed that they must get there early. He was somewhat dismayed to hear that the Provincial Governor was taking an interest in the match. If he had sanctioned it, upsetting the arrangements would not be easy. Only the offer of a greater contest would persuade him to agree to a change. Yi Wan could only hope that his name would be known here, and that Master Cho Ta Hung would accept his challenge. But even if Cho Ta Hung declined, Yi Wan had decided what he would do.

'Where has the animal come from?' he asked. 'Is it wild?'

'It was captured last year, and has been kept in a zoo in the city.'

A city that could boast a zoo would be of no mean size, Yi

Wan thought, and its Governor a man of no mean importance. But he left further questioning to Hi Peng. From the landlord's answers, he learnt that an arena had been especially built for the event, and he learnt too of Cho Ta Hung's reputation. The master could bend iron bars. He could smash rocks with his bare hands. He had killed three challengers. His finger tips were hardened until they were like the beak of a bird. He had even pecked a hole in the wall of a cell with them.

But these stories did not dismay Yi Wan. Some of the information was just legend, but in any case, Yi Wan had the inner knowledge that each time he cared about the distress of a living creature, he shared in the compassion of the Lord Buddha, and for that moment, he linked himself with the eternal Tao. So he went to bed calm, and slept as if the morrow brought no peril.

Twenty

Yi Wan and his party arrived in Tai-Po in the middle of the morning. It was essential that they see the Governor as early as possible.

It was clear from the moment they entered the town that Tai-Po was in festive mood. Already the streets were milling with people, and there was a thriving market, with stalls selling souvenir models of the tiger and of Cho Ta Hung, in addition to their normal wares. People had come in from the country round about, knowing that if the Master could do what he claimed, they would have a story to tell their grandchildren. They would have seen a living legend.

In the central square, Yi Wan paid special attention to the arena. It was decked with bunting and flags, with a high seat for the dignitaries, and the contest area was a pit twelve feet deep, so that spectators would be protected. He was not happy to see that the floor was covered with soft sand which would inhibit speedy movement.

When they enquired about accommodation, they were refused four times, before they found an inn that could take them. At others the answer was the same. 'Did they not know of the special event that had brought men from far and near?'

Their next task was to see the Governor. If he had sanctioned the contest, only he could countermand it. Yi Wan took only Hi Peng with him on this delicate mission, and was glad when they were granted an audience on the strength of his qualifications.

The Provincial Governor was a short, bald-headed man,

rather round in figure, but younger than Yi Wan had expected.

He acknowledged their bows when they entered, with an inclination of his head.

'So you too are a Wu Shu master,' he said without preamble, 'and you teach in Changan?'

'That is so, Your Excellency. Hi Peng is one of my senior pupils.'

'And you think that Cho Ta Hung is a fraud?'

'I did not say that, Your Excellency. All I can say is that I do not believe any man versus animal contest is fair, because the man knows what is coming and the animal does not.'

'A reasonable observation,' the Governor conceded. 'But what do you want me to do? The town is on holiday to watch this trial. People have travelled from miles around.'

'I will give them a spectacle,' Yi Wan answered. 'I will fight Cho Ta Hung, and if I succeed in defeating him, I will prove that the other contest would have been faked.'

'You speak very confidently. Do you know Cho Ta Hung, or anything of his record?'

'I have heard some details.'

'He has defeated the best in Southern China, not once but a dozen times. You may think he is a middle-aged man, and compared with you, he is, but he has that much more experience, and he is still in his prime. He trains daily, and he has been doing special preparation for this event. He knows that he is risking his life, entering the arena with a tiger. He will be at the peak of his form.'

'I am still prepared to challenge him.'

'Well, a master cannot refuse a challenge from another master with your credentials. What exactly do you propose?'

'Your Excellency, before the contest with the tiger, I will fight Cho Ta Hung. If I win, the tiger becomes my property. If I am defeated, the original spectacle may go ahead.'

'Fair enough. Wait in the ante-chamber. My servant will bring you some refreshment, and I will summon Cho Ta Hung.'

Dismissed from the presence, Hi Peng and Yi Wan relaxed on padded benches in a side room, and a man-servant brought them tea. Yi Wan knew that he had got over the first hurdle. The Governor had not acted entirely without self-interest. He had seen at once that what was on offer was two contests instead of one. This would be a bonus to offer the crowd, and it would increase his popularity. Even if Yi Wan was defeated, it could not affect the Governor's reputation in any way. Probably most of the spectators would like to see Yi Wan beaten by their local man.

About half an hour later, Yi Wan and Hi Peng were recalled to the Governor's room. Now another man was with him, Cho Ta Hung.

'So this, Excellency, is the man who says I am a fraud?'

His sneering eyes turned disdainfully upon Yi Wan, appraising his slight figure and youthful appearance.

'This is Master Yi Wan,' the Governor said, judicially.

In a flash, Cho Ta Hung aimed a flurry of blows and kicks at Yi Wan, but despite his relaxed appearance, Yi Wan was prepared, and using the soft evasive techniques that Master Su had taught him, he swivelled his body out of the way.

The Governor smiled.

'You will have to do better than that, Cho Ta Hung.'

'And I shall. So first I am to fight this upstart at three in the afternoon, and when I have finished with him, I will be allowed to make my attempt on the great feat that earned my Master his name.'

'That is so,' the Governor agreed.

Dismissed from the presence of the Governor, Yi Wan and Hi Peng returned to their lodgings.

'All is arranged,' Hi Peng told the others. 'Now the Master must rest.'

If the streets had seemed busy that morning, they were even more crowded in the afternoon. The earth around the arena had been tiered into terraces, so that everyone would have a good view, and already stewards were seating the spectators according to their rank and class.

The marshalls had been warned of the extra contest, however, and Yi Wan and his party were taken straight to a dressing room, where he changed into the loose-fitting trousers and jacket, secured by a sash round the waist, that was the traditional fighting garb.

Just before the Governor arrived, attendants wheeled a low trolley into the arena. On it was a cage, and inside the tiger. The beast lay with his head on his paws, looking placidly around. It had no idea what was happening, and Yi Wan guessed at once that it had become accustomed to seeing human beings outside the bars of its enclosure, during the year it had been kept in the zoo. The attendants dragged it right around the arena, so that all might catch a glimpse of the tiger. A murmur of excitement went up.

After the cage had been taken to one side of the arena, Cho Ta Hung entered. He wore a suit similar to Yi Wan's, but whereas Yi Wan had chosen the plain white garments of his school in Changan, Cho Ta Hung chose yellow and red, and had the head of an eagle embroidered on his jacket. Yi Wan guessed that it was the symbol of his school. Like Yi Wan, he was accompanied by his senior pupils.

Noticing Yi Wan on the opposite side of the arena, he spat on the ground with a gesture of derision. The crowd did not know what to make of the presence of two groups in the arena, and it was not until the Governor had taken his place, that the Senior Marshall told them the additional spectacle in store for them.

A murmur of satisfaction ran around. Exhibitions by masters of Cho Ta Hung's standing were rare. Most teachers taught in secret to selected pupils only, and public demonstrations were almost unknown. To see their most famous master in action against another master was a privilege they prized.

'Let battle begin.'

At the Governor's command, the arena steward beckoned Cho Ta Hung and Yi Wan, to come to the centre of the contest area.

'You know the rules,' he said. 'You have agreed to fight to the death, or until one of you is carried unconscious from the arena.'

He knew, as they did, that the latter provision was a mere form of words. No master would surrender, and any injury severe enough to cause loss of consciousness would eventually be a fatal one.

Both Yi Wan and Cho Ta Hung signified assent. The steward raised his right arm, and bringing it down with a sweeping gesture, he called, 'Begin!' and stepped back out of the way.

Yi Wan expected the flurry of attacks that Cho Ta Hung had heaped upon him in the Governor's residence, but the man had seen that he was too great a master to be caught by a sudden rush like that, and he began circling warily, throwing out a lightning strike, now and then. Yi Wan had no difficulty in evading these, and he knew that they were not part of the main attack, but simply a ruse to try out his defences.

He knew too that defence would not be good enough on its own in this situation. As he had been told at Shaolin, defence was only one side of the martial art. Attack was essential to success. He tried a flying kick, but Cho Ta Hung's inside block knocked it aside, and spun him around. He tried the right and left reverse punch combinations, but Cho Ta Hung was familiar with these, and easily avoided them.

To the crowd, the fight was tame, a mere demonstration of punches and kicks and the respective methods of blocking them. After five minutes, they became restless and started shouting for action.

'Come on, Cho Ta Hung! Where is the eagle now? Is he asleep?'

Their shouts stimulated Cho Ta Hung, and he came forward with his known specialty, the whirling arms that flapped with the speed of an eagle's wings, brushing aside any attempt to get through them. Behind this flurry of arms, Cho Ta Hung knew that he was impregnable, and Yi Wan recognized this too. If he made any attempt to deliver a

punch or a kick through that barrier, he could face a broken
arm or leg. And at any moment, Cho Ta Hung's arm could
shoot out in the deadly three-finger strike that so resembled a
bird's beak, and that could penetrate flesh or snap a bone or
pluck out an eye.

There was only one way to deal with this situation, and that
was to stifle the whirring arms. It called for the grappling
techniques of Shaolin, and the courage to go in at all costs.

Cho Ta Hung had clearly never met anyone who would
risk this, and when Yi Wan's arms wrapped around him,
imprisoning him, he responded with a quite ordinary head
butt and a jab at the testicles with his knee. Both these
techniques were so well known and so commonly expected,
that Yi Wan avoided them automatically. Using his hold on
Cho Ta Hung's jacket, he took the master to the ground. The
violence of the fall winded Cho Ta Hung, but he was still
sufficiently in command to roll to one side and avoid Yi Wan's
follow-through attack.

He sprang to his feet, and realizing that the throw had been
accomplished by holds on his jacket, he stripped it off, taking
the sash in his hands. Yi Wan rose as quickly as he did. When
throwing Cho Ta Hung, he had felt the metal hidden in the
fold of his sash, and knew that the master had a yue concealed
there. This was a multi-edged weapon, which, when attached
to a belt or sash, could be flicked out at long range to cut. It
was probable that he had not intended to use this against Yi
Wan, believing that he could defeat the younger man with
unarmed techniques. The weapon was there in case anything
went wrong in his battle with the tiger.

Since Cho Ta Hung now had the advantage of being
stripped to the waist, Yi Wan slipped off his own jacket, so
that he would have the same freedom of movement.

Immediately, a murmur broke out amongst the nearest
spectators, which swelled and was taken up as a great whisper
that ran around the crowd like a wind.

'The marks of Shaolin!'

Yi Wan had forgotten for a moment that on his upper arms

and his chest were burnt for ever the symbols on the sides of the great urn, which he had lifted on his graduation day at the Shaolin monastery.

He was so highly trained that nothing the crowd said or did would distract him. He did not even hear anything outside the arena. He only knew that Cho Ta Hung now held in his arms a long sash to which was attached the most dangerous weapon Yi Wan had ever faced, and that at any moment he could flick it out, and the razor edges would sever muscle and bone.

He went in.

Cho Ta Hung might have been ready, but the shock of realizing that Yi Wan had trained at Shaolin threw him off-balance for the smallest fraction of a second, and in that time, Yi Wan's first knuckle strike to the oesophagus lifted him clean off the ground and smashed his windpipe. Gasping and spluttering he fell on his back, and before he reached the ground, he was dead.

The crowd were stunned by the suddenness of the end, and by the speed with which their master had finally been defeated. There was silence for a moment. Then, as they took it in, a reluctant and half-hearted cheer arose.

Yi Wan stepped back, trying to still the trembling within him. When he had calmed himself, he signed to the attendants, who were waiting by the tiger's cage. They dragged it into the centre of the arena. This was the real moment of testing, when Yi Wan had to prove that the advertised contest was a fake. This would prove whether he was right or wrong.

Quickly and without fear, since an animal would sense fear and be alarmed by it, Yi Wan thrust his arm through the bars, and with his palm stroked the great cat's head. The beast opened its mouth to snarl, but thought better of it, and laid its head on its fore paws.

'Drugged!'

It was the Provincial Governor who spoke the word first. A moment later, it was on every lip.

Twenty-One

'Well, you've won your tiger. Now what are you going to do with him?'

It was the Provincial Governor who put the question, when he received Yi Wan on his dais, before going back to his residence.

'Release him,' Yi Wan answered at once. 'Tigers live in the forest to the south, don't they?'

'Yes, but you had better seek the advice of the zoo-keeper. Who is going to open the door of his cage? Anyway, I had planned a small reception for tonight for Cho Ta Hung. It would please me, if you and your students came instead.'

'We would be delighted, Your Excellency.'

'Well, make what arrangements you wish for your tiger, and we will see you at seven.'

The reception was held in the main hall of the Residence. The Governor and his wife stood just inside the door, bowing to guests as they were announced. Each bowed courteously in return and some were given the privilege of taking the lady's hand. There were seventeen guests apart from Yi Wan's party.

They were served tea with tiny cakes, and divided into groups, which sub-divided and re-formed in different combinations as the evening wore on. Conversation was light and general. Everyone congratulated Yi Wan on his success, but he felt that there was little warmth in their words, and that many would have preferred their own man to win.

He had never met so many beautiful ladies in one room at

the same time. Their court dresses, with the long puffed sleeves, their diamonds and rings, their perfumed and powdered hair set them apart from the people of his world. He was not much good at the small talk that formed the bulk of their conversation. He was better at talking with a few friends on subjects he knew something about.

The gathering seemed to him to be artificial. He would never meet any of these people again. He would not even remember their names tomorrow. The superficialities they exchanged by way of conversation seemed a complete waste of time to him. Yet he knew it had been an act of courtesy on the part of the Governor to invite them, and he was grateful for the honour.

The only man with whom he struck up any rapport was the Chief of Militia.

'We would be honoured if you would stay in this town,' he told Yi Wan. 'Cho Ta Hung was the chief instructor to my officers. Now that he is dead, we need another instructor.'

'I have my own academy in Changan,' Yi Wan replied. 'My students expect me back.'

'Then of course, you cannot let them down.'

The officer understood loyalty, and Yi Wan respected him for this.

In the morning, he had formulated his plans for the tiger's release. He had already told the zoo-keeper to feed it but not water the animal, and he would repeat this process before they set out for the jungle. Thus the animal would arrive thirsty, and if released near a water-hole, its first instinct would be to slake its thirst. On this, Yi Wan intended to rely, when he opened the cage. He did not tell the others about his plan, because he did not want to face their arguments.

They went to the zoo very early, and Yi Wan questioned both the proprietor and the keepers several times, to make sure that his instructions had been strictly adhered to. The tiger was certainly alert this morning. The drug had worn off, and it was tearing at a carcass in the corner of its cage. It snarled at their approach.

'Let it finish the meal, before you attempt to load it into the travelling cage,' Yi Wan ordered.

Whilst the animal was eating, he examined the travelling cage. There were gates either end, and inside there was just room for the animal to lie down.

'Show me how the gates work,' he demanded.

'They are hinged at the top,' the keeper explained. 'They fall by gravity, and you slide this bar through the rings at the bottom to hold them shut. If you pull the bar out, the gate is then free, and the tiger can push it open from the inside, and simply walk out.'

Yi Wan lifted the gate several times and allowed it to fall. Then he tried fitting the bar into the rings, and withdrawing it again. He saw that there was a space of about two feet on either side, when the cage was loaded onto the cart, so that the tiger could not reach anyone walking alongside the cart. Nor could it reach the horses in front.

'You may not get your cage back,' Yi Wan was forced to tell the zoo-keeper. 'It depends whether the tiger hangs around or makes off into the wild at once. If I should fail to return it, I will pay the cost.'

'You are very generous, master. Do not worry. We can get other cages, but it is the horses I worry about.'

'They will be safe, and you shall have them back today. How far is it to the jungle?'

'If you travel ten miles due south from the town, you will be in the middle of it. You will find that the road dips into a ravine, but if you follow the wood-cutter's path along the edge of the ravine, you will come to a trackless wilderness, and at any point after that, you can turn into the jungle.'

Ten miles with cart horses on an unmarked road could take three hours, Yi Wan calculated. Then they would need another three hours to return.

'We shall be back well before sunset,' he told the zoo-keeper. 'Now that the tiger has finished eating, can your men coax it into the cage?'

The cart and the travelling cage were backed up against the

main one, and the end gate of the cage was aligned with a similar gate in the permanent cage. Attendants with forked sticks stood by, but Yi Wan signalled to them not to touch the animal.

'There is an easier way than that,' he said. 'Simply drop a side of beef into the far end of the travelling cage.'

'But the animal has already eaten its fill.'

'It will eat more. Do you give me your word that it has not been watered?'

'Yes master. Your instructions have been followed rigorously.'

Yi Wan hoped that he could trust the man. His life would depend on this one simple fact. He was anxious that the tiger should not be enraged at this point, by being prodded into the travelling cage, preferring that it should enter of its own free will, tempted by the food. With a little patience, this was accomplished, and the gate was closed.

'Which way?' Yi Wan asked.

The zoo-keeper pointed, and the little procession of Yi Wan, Hi Peng and their students set out. They all rode horses, and one of the students led the cart-horses.

Soon after they had left the town, they were in wild country with no sign of habitation. As the zoo-keeper had said, the road wound down into a ravine, and they left it, keeping to the heights and the wood-cutter's path. The sun rose quickly, and the heat burned down on them. The smell of the tiger and of the fresh meat in its cage reached Yi Wan, even though he was ten yards in front, leading the way. The tiger was clearly not happy, as the wheels wobbled over the bumpy road, and he snarled at anyone who came near. There was not room for him to stand up, however, and he lay with his head on his paws.

At last, Yi Wan found the place he was looking for, an opening in the jungle foliage, made by the bed of a stream.

'Here,' he said, halting the procession. 'Hi Peng and I will lead the cart horses into the jungle. The rest of you stay with the horses.'

'Be careful master,' one of the students warned. 'There may be other tigers, wolves, lions, snakes.'

'Wild animals and even reptiles tend to flee at the approach of man,' Yi Wan told them, 'but we will be wary.'

Dismounting from his horse, he took the bridle of the first cart horse, and led it forward. The animal whinnied, and did not want to enter the jungle, but with Hi Peng at the head of the second horse, they forced a way for the cart into the dense undergrowth. The trees closed in overhead, and they would have found it impossible to get through the undergrowth at any other point, but the stream was broad and it had worn a path for itself.

After following it for a mile, they came to a point where the stream spread out, forming a small pond.

'This will do,' Yi Wan said. 'Unhitch the horses.'

When the horses were free, Yi Wan turned to Hi Peng.

'Take them back to the others. I will be with you later.'

'What are you going to do, master?'

'Open the cage.'

'No, master,' Hi Peng pleaded. 'Simply pull out the bar, and we will ride away on the horses.'

'The gate may catch. The tiger might not have the sense to realize he is free. Or if he does get out, he may attack the cart horses.'

'But if you stay, master, he will tear you to pieces.'

'He is calm, now that the motion of the cart has ceased. He is gnawing at his bone.'

'Master, I know you are concerned about this beast, or you would never have taken the risks you have to save it, but now you have risked enough. You must think of yourself, Yi Wan, or if not of yourself, then of your pupils. We love you, master.'

Hi Peng felt he must try to reason with Yi Wan, now, because, since Jainu had died, his master had seemed absolutely careless of his own safety. But Yi Wan had made up his mind.

'Please go, Hi Peng,' he said. 'When you are at a safe

distance, I will draw the bar. Wait for me one hour. If I don't come, please do not hunt for me. Go back to Changan. Carry on our school. It is partly your's now, and will be altogether, if I ever go away. And, Hi Peng, if I don't join you, please thank your family for all that they have done for me. I love you all, Hi Peng.'

Hi Peng departed with tears in his eyes. He was convinced that he would not see Yi Wan alive again.

When the last sounds of the horses had died away, Yi Wan waited ten minutes, then drew the bar. He knew that at this stage it was vital that no movement of his should alarm the tiger.

When the animal realized that the gate would now open, it rose on its paws, and began to nose the gate upwards. Without haste, or noise, Yi Wan backed into the pond, and kneeling down, began to drink.

He was outwardly calm, controlling his fear, because fear had a smell that animals could detect, but inwardly he was ready for instant action, if it was called for. This moment was fraught with the most extreme danger. It was worse than being in the arena with Cho Ta Hung, because a man's reactions could be calculated, but an animal's were unknown. Yi Wan had relied entirely on his instincts and the things he had been told by hunters. If on either count, he had been misled, he would be torn to pieces in the next few seconds.

Reaching the ground, the tiger took one look at him, paused in disbelief, then padded into the pool, and began to drink. Yi Wan let out his breath very slowly, in relief. His information was correct.

When the tiger had satisfied its thirst, it looked again at Yi Wan, then at its surroundings, and realizing that it was free, it turned and loped off into the jungle. Yi Wan waited several minutes, before paddling downstream, keeping to the water to cover his scent.

He found Hi Peng and the others waiting.

'Master,' they cried. 'You are safe.'

'Yes, but do not go back for the cart. We will pay the

zoo-keeper for the loss.'

'How did you do it?' Hi Peng asked.

'I have heard,' Yi Wan told them, 'and I believed that animals respect the rights of all other creatures at a water hole, because they know that every animal must drink. It is therefore almost unknown for them to attack even their natural enemies or their prey, whilst they are drinking.'

Only man fails to respect that right, he thought.

Part 3
TUNHUANG

Twenty-Two

Back in Changan, Yi Wan immersed himself in his acupuncture practice, and his teaching at the Wu Shu academy, again. It was his defence against the feeling that he had let Jainu down. Reason told him that he could not have saved her from the cholera. Very few recovered, who were as far gone as she was. But even in other respects, he had not given himself to her as fully as she had given herself to him. His patients and his pupils had occupied a disproportionate part of his time, and deep within him, a tiny bit of his heart had always been Poppy's.

He did not consciously think of her now. It was too painful to remember that Poppy belonged to another man, but the years they had spent together in Tunhuang, and the happiness they had known growing up together, were influences that would be with him for ever.

Late in January, nearly four years after he had settled in Changan, a merchant sought out Yi Wan at his treatment rooms.

'I have not come for your professional services, doctor,' he said. 'But you are Yi Wan, formerly of Tunhuang, aren't you?'

'That is so.'

'Then I have a message for you. Master Li Su is ill, and his wife, Wu Su, has bidden me to tell you, and to ask if you will go back to Tunhuang. The Master is concerned that there is no-one in the town who will take over his medical practice and his school, and he would like to make some arrangement before he dies.'

Before he dies! The words struck a chill at Yi Wan's heart. How could he think of Master Su dying? Su appeared indestructible. But Yi Wan knew that Su had been old on the day he had taken him into his house.

'How long ago were you given this message?' he demanded.

'A month, master. That is the time the journey takes.'

Yi Wan knew from his own travels that this was the truth.

'And are you returning to Tunhuang?'

'My caravan will set out as soon as we have done our business. Perhaps in three days.'

Yi Wan's decision to go back was immediate. He felt that he had let Master Su down by coming away in the first place. It was only his love of Poppy that had forced him to leave, and the feeling that he could not bear to live so near her, without wanting her every moment of his waking life, and without a crippling jealousy of the man who had her as his wife. Now, four years later, those feelings would still have power to hurt him, but he was stronger, and he would find the strength to cope with them. Did not true love want the beloved's happiness? And if Poppy was happy with Gao, should not that be the purest joy to Yi Wan?

But what if she were unhappy? Yi Wan could not think of that, without rage at the unfairness of the system that had taken her away from him. To overcome his anger, he turned his mind to the practical arrangements he must make.

As a friend of Master Su, Wen Di accepted without question Yi Wan's decision to return to Tunhuang.

'It is your duty,' he said. 'I know your patients here are going to miss you, but we will spread them between us. Do you think you will return, or should I engage another assistant?'

Yi Wan did not know how to answer.

'I must stay as long as Master Su needs me,' he said. 'Perhaps he will get better. If not, Tunhuang is where my duty lies. Master Su was a father to me, in my time of need.'

Yi Wan had never told Wen Di his exact relationship with Master Su, and as he told the story now, he was conscious of how much the meeting with Su had altered the direction of his life. If Su had not taken him in, he would have been a beggar, until perhaps, some poor man took pity on him, and let him share the family work on a farm. His professional skill, his status in society, his martial skills, his wealth were all gifts from Master Su.

That same afternoon, the merchant reappeared at Yi Wan's consulting room, and fearful that a change of plan was contemplated, Yi Wan told him brusquely, 'I am not ready to go yet. I must make arrangements. You said in three days time.'

'Of course, master,' the merchant replied. 'I only came to ask if you can direct me to Master Su's son, Pei Su. I was given his address in Tunhuang, but he is not there.'

'You will not find him,' Yi Wan answered. 'He is dead. Did his parents not know this?'

As soon as Yi Wan had put the question, he knew that it was a foolish one. If they had known they would not have sent the merchant to his old address.

'Where were you told to seek him?' he asked.

When the merchant told him, Yi Wan saw that it was in the area where Pei had lived as a student. His parents might even have thought he was resuming his studies. It was Yi Wan who would have to tell them the truth.

He spent his last evening at Changan in Master Peng's house, where he had lived since Jainu had died. This was another family to whom he felt he owed a great debt of gratitude. Master Peng had been a valuable friend from the beginning, and a man of influence when charges were about to be laid against Yi Wan. Madame Peng had always been a gracious hostess, welcoming Yi Wan as if he were her own son. Between them they had given him their children, Hi Peng to be his trusted assistant at the academy, Jainu to be his wife.

Yi Wan played the usual games of 'Go' with the old man, sad that these would probably be the last ones they would ever play together. It seemed that life was made up of meetings and partings, and he hoped that in some unseen way, it all linked together, so that the happiness of the past would not really be gone for ever, but would be part of a perceived and existent whole, outside time.

When Hi Peng returned from the academy, Yi Wan asked him how the practice had gone.

'Satisfactory, master, but we missed you. The pupils all asked me to wish you a safe journey, and to say they hope you will be back.'

'I will try, Hi Peng,' Yi Wan said, but in his heart he felt already that it was unlikely that he would return. 'You have been a good friend, and you are an excellent teacher, Hi Peng. I am leaving the school we have built up together in good hands.'

'Thank you, master.'

'The school is your's now, Hi Peng. You helped to develop it, and this is just.'

Knowing that it would be impossible to hire horses, when it was uncertain that he would ever return, Master Peng bought two young animals, and presented them to Yi Wan as a parting gift.

'They will carry your belongings, and will enable you to keep up with the caravan without imposing on the merchants.'

Once again, Yi Wan was in his father-in-law's debt, and with sadness in his heart, he left Changan in a snowstorm.

The caravan he had joined consisted of twenty traders and forty-three camels. These ungainly two-humped Bactrian camels could each carry a load of four hundred pounds. They were laden with silks, the main export of Changan at that time to Europe. The traders were all mounted on horses. Three or four semi-wild dogs accompanied the party. They did not seem to belong to anyone in particular, but everyone fed them, and they were tolerated for the warning of attack that they would give by night.

Each day, the caravan advanced forty miles. The snow which had been falling when they left Changan was not continuous, and tended to lie only on the hills. The trail, which frequently dipped into gorges, was free of ice or snow.

Yi Wan felt that it was fortunate he was travelling in Winter. During the summer months, water had to be carried in goatskin bags, since supplies were few and far between. True, the night temperature was sub-zero, but sharing a tent with a dozen other men, Yi Wan was kept warm.

The traders with whom he was travelling were all of Persian origin, and they spoke little Chinese, so that communication with them was not easy. They were rough men, and spent most of their evenings playing Kalahari around the camp fire. It was a gambling game, and consisted of trying to move pegs into the opponent's receptacle. It was one of the oldest known games on the Silk Road. Princes gambled for slave girls, and merchants for precious stones or for favoured stalls in the market place. Yi Wan held himself aloof from this. His one thought was to reach Tunhuang as soon as possible.

Although he tried to remember the route along which he had been taken as a child captive, he could not be sure that this was the same one. The landscape had no familiar features. They branched north, away from the mountains, and for some days were crossing a flat plain, which stretched to the horizon in all directions. In Summer, it would be a dust-bowl, treeless, and with only the barest scattering of scrub grass to sustain any form of life. Now, in Winter, it was simply a wind-swept barren waste.

When he saw mountains on the southern horizon, he knew they were approaching Tunhuang. He wondered what he would find there.

It was early Spring when they approached the town, and the light was quite different from that on the Summer day, when Yi Wan had arrived there thirteen years earlier. Then it had been golden. Now a piercing silver brightness lit up the adobe walls of the houses, and the new green foliage on the trees seemed to have a translucent quality. Everything looked fresh, as if it had been painted that day, but it was the same town that he remembered.

When they were within sight of the houses, Yi Wan said goodbye to his travelling companions, and spurred his horse ahead, eager to reach Master Su's residence and to hear the news.

A strange girl opened the door to him, reminding him that this would have been Poppy's duty, but of course the girl was not Poppy, though she was a pretty little thing, and Yi Wan wondered if she too were a bond-servant, paying off her father's debts.

'I will call the gardener to take your horses, master,' she said. 'Then please come in. You are expected.'

That he was not only expected but welcome, Yi Wan discovered the next minute, when Madame Su came into the hall, holding out her arms to receive him with a hug.

'Yi Wan!' she exclaimed. 'Is it really you? We have heard so many stories about you, since you left, and now you are back. For good, I hope.'

'I do not know, Madame,' Yi Wan answered, loath to commit himself, until he knew the exact situation in Tunhuang. 'I will stay as long as I am needed, of course.'

'I know you will, and you will always be needed, I am afraid. Here is the groom for your horses. He will bring in your baggage, when he has stabled them.'

'Is Tai Do no longer here?' Yi Wan asked, seeing that the man who came was a stranger.

'Tai Do is dead,' Madame Su answered. 'He was an old man when you were living here, and you have been away four years.'

'And Xi Hang?'

'She is still with us.'

'And Master Su?'

Yi Wan was leaving the more important names in his enquiry to the last, unconsciously putting off hearing what he feared might be bad news.

'Li Su is weakening. He is an old man too. He has been in his bed for several weeks.'

'And can nothing be done?'

'He is a doctor, Yi Wan, like you are. He knows the symptoms. Something must carry off old men. Usually it is difficulty with their breathing. Or you could say simply old age.'

'When shall I be able to see him?'

'As soon as you are refreshed and fed. I will tell him you have arrived.'

The girl showed Yi Wan to his room. It was the same one that he had before, and nothing was changed. Yi Wan did not think now that this had been Pei's room and that this was where he had raped Poppy. He could think of nothing else but Master Su's illness, and of the terrible news he would have to give them about Pei's death.

'What is your name?' he asked the girl, suddenly.

'Kolya, master,' she answered shyly.

'Did you replace Poppy here?'

'I do not know Poppy,' the girl answered. 'I came here two years ago.'

Of course, Yi Wan thought. He could not expect anyone to know much about Poppy. She had left this house under a cloud, because of Pei. His parents would have wanted to forget the matter. Yet it was only they or perhaps Xi Hang, who would be able to tell him about her. He longed to ask and at the same time he dreaded what he might be told, because he had known, as soon as he came through the door, that his love for her was as strong as ever, and the hurt that she was someone else's wife would torture him still.

When the groom brought his luggage to the room, Yi Wan washed and changed, and tried to put her out of his mind. The only way he would be able to take up life here was by coming to terms with the fact that Poppy was married and could never be his. At this moment, he should be concentrating on something much more difficult, the necessity to tell Madame Su and Li Su that he had killed their son. When they heard that, there might be no question of his remaining in their house.

When he went down to the living room, Xi Hang was presented to him.

'So you are back, Yi Wan?' she said.

'Yes.'

There was so much that he wanted to say to her, because, during his adolescence, Xi Hang had been almost a mother to him, but the time was not now. After a few formal words, Xi Hang left the room, and Kolya served the meal. Madame Su and Yi Wan ate alone. Master Su did not get up.

It was in the early afternoon that Yi Wan was taken into the Master's presence, and he was shocked at Su's appearance. Li Su had shrunk, until his face was like parchment stretched over the bones, having an almost translucent quality. He lay back on his pillows, a bowl of soup untouched at his bedside. His breathing came in rasping gasps. Only his eyes, big and smiling and wonderful, gave the impression of life to his face.

Yet, he roused himself on his elbow, when Yi Wan went in, and would have bowed had he been standing up, in the courtesy of one master to another. Instead, Yi Wan went forward and took his hand between both of his.

'Master,' he said. 'Master, I have come.'

Choked with sorrow, Yi Wan could say no more for a few moments, and Su held onto his hands, as he slowly lowered his head to the pillows again.

'Sit down, Yi Wan,' he said. 'There is a stool there, isn't there? I heard that you fought Cho Ta Hung, in order to save a tiger. Tell me about that.'

'If it will not tire you, master.'

'What if it does tire me now? I shall have long enough to rest, when I am dead.'

'You must not speak of dying, master.'

But Master Su only smiled, and to please him, Yi Wan related his story.

'It was your compassion that attracted me to you in the first place,' Su said, when Yi Wan had finished. 'You still have that kind of love. But you picked a bigger cat this time.'

He was laughing quietly to himself, and Yi Wan wondered how he could ever begin to tell Su about Pei. But he must.

'I am sorry that I have some terrible news for you,' he began.

'That you must go away again? That you cannot stay?'

'No, about Pei.'

'Ah yes.'

Master Su's look of resignation made Yi Wan hope that it would not be such a shock after all. Su clearly was prepared to hear that some ill had befallen his son. But he could not know what ill.

'Pei is dead,' Yi Wan said gently.

'How, and when?' Master Su asked, after a pause.

'Master, he and two thugs attacked me, when I was on my way home, one night. He died in the fight. I killed him, Master. How can I ask or expect you to forgive me?'

Su made the slightest gesture with his hand, to stay Yi Wan's words.

'Tell me why he attacked you,' he said quietly.

Knowing that Pei's way of life, and the profession in which he had been engaged, must hurt Master Su still further, Yi Wan would have softened the blow, if he could, but, as on the very first day he had met Su, he felt now that the Master would see through any untruth or fabrication. Now, as much as then, he saw beyond words to the truth that was beyond them. It would be impossible to deceive him.

Briefly, he told the master about Suzie, about Pei's profession, about his anger that Yi Wan was interfering with the girls, by advising them of the health risk they ran in their nightly work.

Su listened in silence, and Yi Wan was afraid that he had hurt his master beyond forgiveness. He had repaid kindness and love by killing Su's only son. Could any parent forgive that? Of course, Yi Wan knew that the case was not as simple as that. He had not really been given a choice. When Pei Su had attacked him, it had been Pei's life or his.

Master Su understood this, without telling.

'I was always afraid for Pei,' he said, when Yi Wan had finished. 'He had his own values. They were not mine or his mother's.'

He seemed exhausted, but whether by the news he had just

heard, or by the effort of talking, Yi Wan could not decide. He waited for Su to speak.

'Do not blame yourself, Yi Wan,' the master said, at last. 'I will tell my wife. She will understand. But leave me now, if you will. I am so very tired.'

It was the last time Yi Wan saw Master Su alive. He died during that night.

Twenty-Three

The next few days were filled with the obsequies. Madame Su accepted her loss with the outward calm of one who had long known the end was near, and who had prepared herself to meet that time. The household mourned, but it was a dignified inward sorrow rather than an outward display of grief. This was exactly what Master Su would have wished, Yi Wan thought.

He stood by, ready to carry out any duty, or to run any errand that helped Madam Su, but he did not intrude on her private sorrow, and kept to his room as much as possible, since the weather was too inclement to wander about the garden or the town. He wondered what the future now held for him. Would Madame Su still want him to stay, and to carry on Li Su's work in the town? Had Master Su told her about Pei?

He had his answers to these questions on the day after the funeral.

'Come and talk with me this morning,' Madame Su told him, and when Yi Wan presented himself in the sitting room, she closed the door and came straight to the point.

'You know that it was my husband's wish that you should take over his school and his acupuncture practice?'

'I was told that he wanted to make an arrangement to that effect. That is one of the reasons I came back, but it was by no means the only reason. When I heard he was ill, I felt that I must see him again. I felt that I had let him down by going to Changan in the first place. You know that it was because of

Poppy. I could not bear to live here, where every part of the house would remind me of her, when I knew she could not be mine.'

'And you married in Changan?'

'Yes. The daughter of Master Peng, who was one of my best friends in the city, and who not only helped me to establish my Wu Shu school, but who also protected me by his influence when I was in trouble with the Tangs.'

'Where is your wife now?'

'She died, in the cholera epidemic.'

'So you are free to return to Tunhuang, permanently.'

'Yes.'

'Li Su has left you the practice and the school,' Madame Su told him. 'This is a big house. He wishes you to live here, if you agree, and to carry on the medical practice as in the old days. It will also be convenient for you in the supervision of the school, since it is in the building behind the house. I am to have a suite of rooms in the house, and to receive a percentage of your fees during my lifetime. When I die, everything will be yours absolutely.'

Yi Wan was overwhelmed by the extent of Master Su's generosity. He had expected that he would have been given the work as a paid employee of Madame Su, since there was no-one else with his qualifications in the area, but he had never expected to be made the eventual owner of everything.

He wondered if Madame Su knew about Pei.

'Did he tell you about your son?' he asked.

'Yes.'

Her mother's natural feelings prevented her saying any more for a few moments. Then she added, 'You must forgive yourself, Yi Wan. Pei was my son. I loved him as a mother does love her child, but he was a disappointment to us, even when he was little. He was disobedient, cruel, what other people would call "a little horror". We hoped he would grow out of these traits. When he was only sixteen, he mis-used the skills his father had taught him, to fight a boy in the town. Master Su stripped him of his grades, and sent him to

Changan to study for the civil service. We hoped student life would exhaust the wildness within him, and that he would settle down. But it was not so. He did not apply himself to his studies. He failed his exams. Yet, when he went to Changan for the second time, we had hopes that he would find employment in some honourable business. His father gave him some addresses of friends who might help him.'

'I am sorry that he did not do this,' Yi Wan answered.

'I must confess to you now, that when Li Su brought you home as a twelve year old boy, I was jealous of you,' Madame Su went on. 'Li was so taken with you. I know he did not let you see, but from the moment he brought you into the house, you became in effect his son. He had already decided that Pei would never reform, and his plans began to revolve around you, not around Pei.'

'How old was Master Su?' Yi Wan asked.

He had never been told, not even at the funeral.

'Eighty,' Madame Su answered. 'We had been married sixty years, but we did not think of age. I am seventy-six. I married at sixteen. I rejoice that I am old, Yi Wan, because I know it will be that much sooner that I shall join Li Su again.'

'And you wish me to stay here, too?'

'Of course. The patients and the students need you. I am afraid, however, that you will find the Martial Arts school greatly reduced in size. For the past six months, Li was not able to give it the attention that was needed. Tuition had to be entrusted to older pupils. The acupuncture practice is still flourishing, however. When Li Su found it necessary to conserve his energy, he chose to give what he had to the healing art.'

This reflected Master Su's values so exactly that it brought him alive to Yi Wan again.

'Then I will go over to the academy this evening and see what is happening, and in the morning, I will open up the consulting rooms again.'

'Our present gardener has maintained Tai Do's herb garden. You will find he can supply all the samples you need.'

'Thank you.'

Bowing politely, Yi Wan left the widow's presence, and went to his room. He needed to adjust to his new position. He had been relatively well-to-do, when he had left Changan, because his fees for consultations in the capital added to the profits from the Wu Shu academy had mounted up. Now, however, he was even better off. He had a ready-made home, an acupuncture practice, and the building and equipment to develop an existing martial arts school, and all this without laying out any of his capital. He was stepping into an established business, and his only regret was that it was Pei's inheritance that he was stepping into.

He wondered what had gone wrong in that young man's life. Had he been spoilt by his mother? Or been too sternly disciplined by his father? Or was it some natural weakness of character that had turned Pei into the wrong paths? No-one could tell, and Yi Wan felt it was now fruitless to speculate. All he could do was to try to be worthy of the faith which Master Su had shown in him.

When he went to the Wu Shu academy that evening, he found twenty students there. Practice was already in progress, but the young man in charge immediately called a halt, and turning to Yi Wan, bowed on behalf of the class.

'I am Chee Yuan, Master. On behalf of the class, I welcome you.'

Yi Wan bowed in return, and after introducing himself, he asked them to continue practising.

'I will watch for a while,' he said, 'and then, when you have finished your exercises, we can sit down and discuss how you would like to see the class develop.'

He took his seat, not on the raised dais, where Master Su had usually sat with honoured guests, but on a bench at the side of the hall.

Chee Yuan continued to put the students through their routine. They were practising the usual blocks and kicks, moving down the room to numbers, turning, and coming back again. Their standard was good, as Yi Wan had expected it would be. Any school that had enjoyed the privilege of being taught by a master like Li Su did not deteriorate immediately the master left.

Watching them, Yi Wan could see Su's influence in all the movements. Everyone was learning his swift evasive turns; everyone had the same lightning response to an attack. The whole system was gentle, based more on the need to avoid being hurt than on the desire to hurt. It was almost purely defensive in structure, but Yi Wan knew from experience that if need arose, the same system could be adapted to attack. Master Su had won his own reputation many years ago, as a hard fighter.

When practice was over, Yi Wan asked them to sit down, and they ranged benches in a semi-circle around him.

'Are you the only students now?' he asked.

'Yes,' they agreed.

'And it is obvious that you have all been training for some years. Later, I will speak with you individually, and learn your names, where you are from, and your object in training. But first I would like to talk to Chee Yuan about the course. I myself trained under Master Su, and I want to carry on teaching his style, because I have found it useful in reality. It has saved my life more than once. I would also like to introduce some of the techniques I learnt at Shaolin. I hope that will be acceptable.'

A murmur of agreement told Yi Wan that this was so, and dismissing them he told Chee Yuan to come to the house, as soon as he had washed and changed.

In his room, Yi Wan offered Chee Yuan tea.

'You have gained your teaching certificate?' he asked, as soon as his guest was settled.

'Yes. Master Su gave me my degree, just before he retired. I was the last person to receive such a qualification from him.'

'He did not give out many,' Yi Wan answered. 'But even from my brief observation this evening, I could see why he thought so highly of you. How old are you, Chee Yuan?'

'Twenty-two, master.'

'And how long have you studied here?'

'Twelve years, master. When you first came, I was in the juniors class, but you would not have noticed me, in particular, because there were so many in the class, and of course, you did your own training with the seniors.'

Yi Wan could not remember Chee Yuan, but it was as he had said. Twelve years ago, the classes were so full that no-one knew everyone else.

'Numbers have fallen drastically, I see,' he said. 'Do all the pupils we have now reside in the town?'

'Half of them come from other cities, and lodge here, while they are completing their training. They hope to qualify and either to open their own schools when they go home, or to take up posts which are awaiting them. Some are going to be body-guards to officials, or to traders who have to travel a lot.'

'What about the pupils who are from Tunhuang?'

'They are all pupils who joined on Master Su's personal invitation. Usually the parents had approached him. As you will know, he was very strict about who might be admitted to the school. Out of a dozen who applied, he might only accept one.'

'Do you train during the day, or only in the evenings?'

'There are afternoon classes. The hall is open in the morning for private practice, or for those who want to use the punching boards and bags.'

'Chee Yuan, will you be my chief assistant? I am going to carry on the acupuncture practice that Master Su established. I shall therefore only be free to teach in the evenings. But I found that this arrangement has worked very well in my school, in Changan. My assistant took all the day time classes and some private pupils. I taught only in the evenings, and when class was over, I did private practice with my assistant. We could do the same if you wish.'

When he was talking to Chee Yuan about what happened in his Changan school, Yi Wan remembered Hi Peng with gratitude. He had spent hundreds of hours practising with Hi Peng. No two people could spend that time together without becoming firm friends. If Hi Peng had been able to come to Tunhuang, nothing would have given Yi Wan so much pleasure as to welcome him. But Hi Peng's place was with his family. He was the only child they had now, and the Changan school needed him.

'It would be an honour to assist you, master,' Chee Yuan answered. 'Master Su has spoken of you, so often.'

'You have no other post waiting for you, nor any other call on your time?'

'I live in Tunhuang, master. My parents keep a store that sells farm implements and seeds. We are not of the Shih or even of the Nung class. We are of the Shang.'

'That is no matter,' Yi Wan said. 'The old distinctions are becoming less important, and in the practice hall, it is dedication, ability, and having the right spirit that counts.'

He knew, however, that for Master Su to have accepted a student from the shop-keeper class meant that the boy must have shown outstanding talent and exceptional character.

'So you will live at home, and come to the academy daily?'

'If that is your wish, master.' ·

'I would, of course, like to see the school expand.'

'That will follow now that you are here,' Chee Yuan told him. 'It has only declined since Master Su became ill. I do not have the reputation needed to attract new entrants, but once it is known that you are in charge of studies, some of those who have left will return, and others will apply.'

The following morning, Yi Wan went to the consulting room immediately after breakfast. The girl who acted as practice attendant was waiting for him.

'I have booked in three appointments for this morning,' she said. 'I hope that is acceptable.'

'How did the patients know that I would be here?'

'They are all people who have been before. They were at Master Su's funeral, and they learned then that you would be carrying on his work. Word will quickly spread around the town. You will never be short of patients.'

Yi Wan took the record cards she gave him, and prepared

to see the first patient.

By the end of the week, he had settled into a routine that was very little different from the pattern of his life in Changan. He treated patients by day; he taught Wu Shu in the early evenings; he practised with Chee Yuan in the late evenings. He saw little of Madame Su, but he knew that she had forgiven him for killing her son.

Gradually, he settled down. The fierce punishing disciplines he had forced upon himself when Jainu had died became part of his past. He accepted life, and he accepted himself, knowing that he had made mistakes, knowing that he had withheld himself from Jainu, but knowing too that he ought not to go on blaming himself unmercifully. Neither Master Peng, nor Madame Peng nor their son had for one second accused him of responsibility for Jainu's death. Even she herself had forgiven his neglect of her, in the joy of finding that she was to bear his child. That she had not lived long enough for the child to be born was no-one's fault. Cholera's choice of victims was haphazard.

Yi Wan often saw his cat, and always remembered that it was not his cat, but that it was he who belonged to the animal. This was made clear to him by the way the cat reminded him that it had a will of its own. It would never come into the house, though he tried to tempt it up to his room. It preferred the stable where they had once slept together. Now a powerful tomcat, it came to the kitchen door to be fed each morning, but did not want Yi Wan to pet it, except on rare occasions, when it seemed to crave a little sympathy, and would climb all over him.

You don't really need me, Yi Wan thought. You have managed for four years without me. But I need Poppy, he added, in his mind. He tried not to think of her, but his love for her still hurt. He knew it was wrong to want another man's wife, but he wanted Poppy, with all his being. It was not just a physical wanting. He could have appeased the lusts of his body with another woman. But his longing for Poppy was a spiritual desire for union with the only girl who had ever meant anything to him at the deepest level.

Sometimes, it shocked Yi Wan to realize that this was how he felt, because he would know in such moments that he ought never to have married Jainu. He had not been fair to her. Her attraction for him had been physical. He had used her for sexual satisfaction, but his heart had always belonged elsewhere.

For weeks, he dared not ask about Poppy, but at last curiosity forced him to speak to Xi Hang.

'Poppy went home,' she said, as if Yi Wan had forgotten what had happened.

'Yes, but where is she now? Did she marry Gao?'

'Who is Gao? How should I know?'

'Gao is the farmer whom her parents had arranged she should marry. He had agreed to honour his bargain, even though she was carrying Pei Su's child.'

Yi Wan's words seemed to stir Xi Hang's memory.

'She did not have Pei's child,' she told him.

'What are you saying, Xi Hang?'

'Yes, what am I saying? I do not know all the facts. I only know stories I hear in the market.'

'Tell me these stories, Xi Hang.'

'They say that Poppy had a miscarriage, and that then her husband-to-be refused to marry her. He was a good man, by all accounts. He would have taken her and Pei's child, and they would have had more children of their own. But when Poppy had a miscarriage and it was said that as a result she could not bear any more children, he asked for the annulment of the bargain he had made with her parents. A farmer needs a big family to work on the land.'

'So where is Poppy now?'

'Probably working on her parents' farm.'

Twenty-Four

From the moment he knew that Poppy was unmarried, Yi Wan's one thought was to seek her out, but caution made him temper the wild hopes that flooded his mind. Even if she had not married Gao, some other arrangement might have been made. He had been away four years, and was he not presumptuous in thinking that she would remember him or want him? They had parted when he was twenty and she only a year older. She would have widened her circle of acquaintances since. She might not like him any more.

In any case, he had already been married. What would Poppy think of that? What could she think but that he had easily forgotten her, though he knew this was not true, and that he had never forgotten her, nor ever would.

There was a further factor which he knew he ought to take into account. Poppy had been a bond-servant in this house. How would she feel at coming back as its mistress? And how would Madame Su and Xi Hang receive her? If he married Poppy, and sometimes he dared to think this might be possible, he might have to re-think all his plans for the future. He might have to throw away all the opportunities that were now presented to him, and disappoint yet again all Master Su's hopes for him.

Yet none of these considerations altered the fact that he loved Poppy, and that he wanted to see her at once. Supposing that even now it was too late, and her father had found another suitor for her! The thought that procrastination could still rob him of Poppy made Yi Wan act at once. He approached Madame Su.

'You will remember Poppy, Madame Su?' he asked, when they met at dinner that evening.

'Yes, Yi Wan.'

There was a coldness in her tone that warned him his proposal might be even more unwelcome than he had thought.

'I have heard that she is still unmarried.'

'I am not surprised. Men are not too ready to accept a girl in her condition.'

'But it was Pei's fault,' Yi Wan protested. 'You know that he forced himself on her.'

'There has to be a certain amount of complicity in these matters. Poppy was a pretty little thing and she knew it. Pei was only human.'

'I cannot believe that Poppy encouraged him.'

Yi Wan had difficulty in restraining the anger he felt at the injustice of her words.

'Well, of course, you are entitled to think what you like.'

'Madame Su, I love Poppy. I am going to seek her out, and if she agrees, I am going to marry her.'

Madame Su's eyebrows rose in astonishment.

'What I am asking you is whether, if this comes about, I can bring her here as my bride, or whether I should take her away, and try to build a life with her somewhere else?'

Madame Su took her time in replying.

'It was Li Su's dearest wish that you should take over his work here,' she said, at last. 'Nothing should interfere with that. If you are thinking that I would not like to see Poppy as mistress of this house, that is thoughtful of you, but I do not think it would worry me unduly. I should simply keep entirely to my own quarters. We can live quite separately, because my wing can be sealed off, if you wish. I do not know how Xi Hang will feel about taking orders from a girl to whom she once gave the orders. That is something you would have to work out. It might be acceptable, because we never treated Poppy as a servant. We all liked her and regarded her almost as part of the family.'

All except Pei Su, Yi Wan thought. To him she was a possession, to be treated as he wished.

'Then it will not offend you, if I approach Poppy? And if she marries me, you will still wish me to remain here?'

'My wish is that Li Su's hopes for you should be fulfilled. I also want to see you happy, Yi Wan.'

The next morning, Yi Wan told the gardener to have horses ready, and as soon as the practice attendant arrived, he told her to re-schedule his appointments for that day. Then he rode to Chee Yuan's home.

'Will you come with me, Chee Yuan? I want to visit a farm out in the country. Is there some senior pupil whom we can leave in charge of classes for today?'

'Shu Dian.'

'Where does he live? Can we find him at once? But I see you have not breakfasted, Chee Yuan. Give me his address, and I will make the arrangement with him. Then will you come with me immediately after?'

'If you wish, master.'

After calling on the student, who lived in the next street, Yi Wan returned, leading a horse for Chee Yuan.

'Where are we going, master?' the man asked, as they mounted.

Yi Wan told him.

His thoughts went back to that earlier time, when he had set out on this road with So Yeng, and he found himself praying that this time his mission would be more successful.

The road was dusty, but Spring had brought flowers to some of the bushes, and what little vegetation there was had a fresh green-ness about it. They rode in silence and in single file, because two riders abreast presented a better target to bandits. But Yi Wan was not thinking of bandits that morning, and confident of the prowess of both Chee Yuan and himself, he was not nervous of attack.

They made good progress, and turned off the main road about midday.

'Not many more miles,' Yi Wan told Chee Yuan.

'That is good master. The horses will not keep up this pace, in the heat of the afternoon.'

When they reached the farm, there was no sign of life, and Yi Wan's heart sank. Had the family moved away? Had another dry season robbed them of possession of the land?

He dismounted, and hammered on the closed door of the dwelling. It was a long time, before an old woman answered, and then she opened the door just a few inches.

'Madame Quin?' Yi Wan enquired politely.

'Yes, master.'

Recognising his status by his dress, the old woman opened the door wider.

'You must forgive me, master. I am alone in the house today, and there are bandits around.'

'Where is your husband?'

'He went to the market yesterday. I expect him back this evening.'

'And your daughters?'

'They are tending the flocks in the fields. They will bring them in at sunset.'

'I am Yi Wan. I am from Master Su's household, where Poppy once worked. I would like to speak to Poppy, if I may.'

'You will find her in the fields, with the others.'

The old woman regarded him without curiosity. If she wondered why a young gentleman should seek out her daughter, she did not ask. She simply pointed the way.

'May we leave the horses here? Chee Yuan will attend to them and we will pay you for hay and whatever is needed.'

'Of course.'

'Stay here,' Yi Wan told his companion. 'I will be back.'

'If you would like a meal,' the old woman said, 'we have only soup and bread, but you are welcome.'

Yi Wan thanked her, and accepted the invitation on behalf of Chee Yuan. He did not feel he could eat or drink anything himself, until he had learned his fate, and if Poppy could not be his, he wondered if he would ever have interest in such ordinary things as food and drink again.

He walked quickly towards the hill and the clump of trees where he had seen Poppy with her sisters on his last visit. They were not in the same place today, but tiny dots on the horizon showed him that the cattle were grazing much nearer the foothills. He ran on.

When he came up to their picnic site, he would not have recognized Poppy. Clad in a coarse one-piece garment that reached to her ankles, and with a straw sunhat covering her black hair, she bent over a wood fire, on which a black pot was boiling. Her two sisters were farther on, controlling the wanderings of a herd of cows, by gently swishing them with thin branches.

'Is it you, Poppy?' Yi Wan asked, when the small face looked up at the sound of his footsteps.

Poppy immediately looked away without answering, and Yi Wan saw that she was ashamed that he should find her thus, the drudge who did the camp duties, while her sisters did the lighter work.

'It is me, Yi Wan,' he went on, though he knew that she had recognized him.

'What do you want, Yi Wan?'

Her voice had the same quality of music in it that had attracted Yi Wan when he had first heard her speak, but her attitude now was one of apathy. She seemed resigned to what she was doing.

'Poppy, look at me. Talk to me. I am told that you did not marry Gao.'

She assented to this.

'He would have taken me if I had been able to bear him further children,' she defended. 'But a wife who cannot have children is useless to a farmer.'

'So you work on your father's farm?'

'What else is there for me?'

'And your sisters?'

'They are both married. Their husbands have joined their farms to our's. We are prosperous now, compared with the time you last came here. We shall never have to give children to be bond-servants again.'

'Leave the fire a moment,' Yi Wan commanded, and taking her wrists, he pulled her to her feet.

Her head reached his chest, and she looked up at him in wonder.

'Poppy, you are not bound to anyone else, are you?'

'No,' she said.

'Then I am asking you, will you marry me?'

'What are you saying, Yi Wan? I cannot have children. Of what use would I be to you?'

'Children are not the only thing in life, or the only reason for marrying. I have loved you, Poppy, ever since we used to study reading together at Master Su's. I loved you even before that, since it was my love for you that made me suggest the lessons. It was the only way I could think of to meet you regularly.'

'And how is Master Su?'

Yi Wan realized then that she did not know the news, or anything about his own present position. She must be wondering what on earth he was doing there.

'Master Su is dead,' he told her, 'and he has left me his school and his medical practice, to carry on. I am back in Tunhuang for good, Poppy, and I want you to marry me. My dearest, the only reason I went away was because I could not bear to be reminded of you, when you belonged to someone else. I have never ceased to think of you, and to want you. Come with me to Tunhuang, Poppy. Be my wife. Please!'

'But what will Madame Su say? And Xi Hang?'

'I am now master of the house in Tunhuang. Madame Su has rooms there, but she will keep to her own quarters and we shall not see much of her. She is happy for you to come. And Xi Hang has always been fond of you. She will welcome you.'

'What will my father say?'

'If he is sensible and wants your happiness, he will give his consent.'

'But you must ask him. He is still head of the household.'

'Everything shall be done in proper ordering, Poppy. Only say that you will have me.'

She still hesitated, and Yi Wan saw that she could not believe that this was happening to her. He remembered then that he had been married. It was his duty to declare this to her.

'When I left you, I went to Changan, I practised acupuncture there, and I set up a Wu Shu school.'

'I heard that you had gone away, Yi Wan.'

'Whilst I was in Changan, I got married.'

Seeing her dismay, he hurried on.

'My wife died in a cholera epidemic. We did not have children.'

'Did you love her?' Poppy asked.

'I loved her, but in a different way to my love for you. If you had been free, Poppy, I would never have looked at another girl. I pictured you with Gao. I thought that our love had no hope of ever finding fulfilment.'

'So you took what happiness you could find. I do not blame you for this, Yi Wan.'

'Now that I am free, I know that you are the only girl I have ever really wanted.'

Her arms slid around him, and pulled him to her, and the next moment, his lips met hers, as he tilted her face up, to kiss her with a passion and intensity that had the love of a dozen years behind it.

'Poppy, Poppy,' he breathed, between kisses. 'I love you. I want you.'

When her sisters returned to the fire for lunch, they looked at Yi Wan curiously, and although they accepted that he was sharing their stew and bread, they kept apart from their sister and did not ask questions.

It was Yi Wan who told them.

'I am going to marry your sister, with your father's permission, of course.'

They giggled like children, and Yi Wan saw that this was something they had never expected for Poppy. Marriages, in their experience, were arranged, as their's had been, and when an arrangement broke down, as Poppy's had done, there was only work in her parents' house for a girl to fall back upon.

'We are going to ask your father as soon as he returns from the market.'

* * *

Yi Wan and Poppy were married three weeks later, and she returned to the house in Tunhuang, where she had been a bond-servant, as its mistress. During that short time, Yi Wan had gained the confidence of patients in his medical practice, and had begun to build up the Wu Shu academy again.

He felt that here he belonged.

Remembering the way Jainu felt he had neglected her, he made up his mind, from the first day of his marriage, that he would not allow Poppy to feel shut out of his life. He arranged his day, so that patients were seen in the early morning and afternoon, Wu Shu practice took place in the late afternoon, and the evenings were entirely Poppy's.

From the first hours of their marriage, they resumed the old happy relationship with each other, rejoicing in just being together, sharing the same activities, even though these were just the mundane tasks of life. Just to be with Poppy, to hear her voice or to touch her hands, gave Yi Wan such exquisite joy that he felt himself the happiest man alive, and at night, when they made love, his joy reached a peak that he knew could never be surpassed. He loved her with every fibre in his body, with his heart and mind and spirit, and in loving her, he knew that he was united with her, and that they were forever one.

Often, when the evenings grew longer, they would sit outside in the herb garden, enjoying the scents and the distant view of the mountains, and Yi Wan would remember how he had first come to this house, and all the kindnesses he had met with since.

He sensed that there was a pattern to his life, and felt that he did not live it of his own volition, but followed some pre-arranged plan. He could not explain many of the things that had happened to him, the cruelty of his parents' death, his capture by the soldiers who had chosen to spare him, but he felt that some Power looked after him, and had guided his escape and brought him to the safety of Master Su's home.

That Power was the Tao, and in those moments when his compassion for the kitten or the tiger, or his love for Poppy filled his heart, he was conscious of his unity with the Tao, and this, not as an intellectual concept, but as a living experience.

Following Poppy into the house, one evening, he was arrested by a rasping mew. He looked down to find his cat looking up at him.

Xi Hang grinned, and without saying anything handed him a dish of meat. Yi Wan set it before the cat. The animal purred as it was eating, just as it had done when a kitten.

'You are still his,' Xi Hang said.

But today, Yi Wan belonged to everyone, to his wife, to his patients, to his students, and to every helpless creature that might need him, and in giving himself to them, Yi Wan found himself, and knew that all was well.